The Black Dog
(A Marcie and Amanda Mystery)

by

Glen Ebisch

This book is fiction. All characters, events, and organizations portrayed in this novel are the product of the author's imagination or are used fictitiously. Any resemblance to actual persons—living or dead—is entirely coincidental.

For information, email **Cozy Cat Press**, cozycatpress@aol.com or visit our website at: www.cozycatpress.com

COZY CAT
PRESS

ISBN: 978-1-939816-15-3
Printed in the United States of America

Cover design by Keri Knutson
http://alchemybookcover.blogspot.com/

1 2 3 4 5 6 7 8 9 10

Dedication: For my wife

Chapter 1

Jerome Kronberg stood at the top of West Peak and looked around him. In the distance to his left he could see the city of Meriden; to his right were the more open spaces of rural western Connecticut. He shivered a little and zipped up his jacket. It was a blustery day in April and the wind was quickly drying the sweat that was on his body from the two-hour climb, which, although not technically difficult, was challenging enough for someone who'd only recently given up an investment adviser's desk for hiking.

As he stood on the peak, he had a sense of being alone and free. He felt his heart sink as he considered the word "freedom." The odds were good that his days of freedom were numbered. Even now the federal prosecutor's office was compiling evidence that would soon result in his arrest for fraud. His attorney had warned him that the only way to avoid significant jail time would be to cooperate with the authorities. He was giving serious consideration to just that, although there was one person who urged him to remain steady. Loyalty, he thought with a smile. Who could expect that from a man who had happily and with a pleasant smile swindled his friends out of millions? Why should there be honor among thieves when there was none among friends?

He took one last survey of the area, watching the gray clouds scudding across the sky to the west and wondering what sort of view he would have from a prison cell. He knew that he wasn't a strong man, and that the fear of incarceration would soon push him in the direction of telling all he knew. He only hoped it was enough. But even being free wouldn't protect him from his victims; they would sue for damages. But there was more danger than that. One of those whom he'd swindled had already openly threatened him. He knew that others who kept their hatred within themselves might eventually prove more dangerous. Was someone out there even now plotting his demise, smiling at revenge about to be fulfilled?

As he started to turn to go back the way he had come, he saw a small black figure run out from the trees and head towards him. A black dog. He knew the story. He should; he'd already seen the dog twice. The first time nothing bad had happened. The second time he'd returned home to find that his partner, Jeffrey Hunter, had committed suicide. The third time you saw the dog, legend said, it meant your own death. His heart pounding in terror, he quickly backed away from the creature that was eagerly running up the slope towards him as if happy to see him, its mouth open but not emitting a sound. Its feet seeming not to touch the ground. A ghostly dog, a sepulchral dog.

His back slammed into an outcropping of rock. To his right was the dog and to the left was the edge of the cliff. He prepared himself to turn, go around the rock, and run back down the mountain. Perhaps you can't outrun death, he thought desperately, but what choice did he have?

As he readied himself to turn and run as he'd never run before, a powerful force struck his right side, propelling him toward the cliff. Before he realized it, he was off the mountain and falling into space.

Chapter 2

Marcie Ducasse sat at her desk at *Roaming New England Magazine,* staring out the window at the cars passing by on Route 1 in Wells, Maine. The Friday morning traffic was relatively light, confined to local commuters. April was too early for much in the way of tourists. In another month it would be pleasant to walk on the beach, Marcie thought. April was generally still too windy and cold, especially in the morning, her favorite time to walk. Although there were days in the winter when she would bundle up and go out on the beach, even in January when the frozen wet sand would crackle under foot.

She was pondering all these things because, to be honest, she was bored. There were still a number of editing chores to be done on the next issue of the magazine, but she wanted more in the way of action. She had spent the entire winter cooped up in the office, never once having the opportunity to go out in the field and investigate a story. There had been plenty of articles about New England history and travel for her to accept and edit, but there had been no tales of the supernatural, at least none that involved recent sightings. So she'd been reduced to summarizing bizarre historical events for the *Weird Happenings* column, which usually made for good reading, but didn't leave any room for out of office research. Marcie was so desperate for action that she'd even spent several hours at home last night poring through all the letters and e-mails she'd received at the magazine in the past six months, hoping for some story of the supernatural that might be suitable for her column and that, more importantly, would require some hands on reporting.

The phone rang. She muttered under her breath. Since they had no funds for a receptionist or a switchboard, the telephone number printed in the magazine for the staff rang on her desk. There was a separate number for advertisements that went through to their one-person business office. But it was Marcie's job to field all the non-marketing calls and decide which had to be forwarded to Amanda Vickers, the managing editor, whose office was down the hall.

"Hello," a woman's voice said when she answered the phone, "I'm trying to reach Marcie Ducasse."

People almost never called for her by name. She felt a momentary rush of apprehension at having such direct contact with the public, almost enough to cause her to say Marcie wasn't in and could she take a message. But she decided that was silly.

"This is Marcie," she said.

"Wonderful, my name is Sheila Little, and I'm a big fan of yours. Or I guess I should say that I'm a fan of your column."

"*Weird Happenings*?"

She never got calls from people who claimed to be fans. Occasionally someone would send a letter or e-mail commenting favorably on an article or offering their own interpretation of a supernatural event. But people never seemed to feel motivated enough to make such direct contact.

"That's right. I love the column. I like the whole magazine, but that column really makes it for me."

"Well, thank you, that's good to hear." Marcie paused, wondering if that was Sheila's only purpose in calling.

"Actually, I wanted to talk to you because an event has happened down here in Comford, Connecticut, that might be of interest to you."

"Where is Comford?"

"About five miles north of Meriden."

Marcie pulled her notebook closer and took out a pen.

"What's the story?"

"Have you heard of Jerome Kronberg?"

Marcie still thought of herself as primarily a journalist; therefore, she made a point of reading the *Boston Globe* and *The New York Times*. So she'd heard the name.

"Wasn't he involved in some kind of financial swindle?"

"Exactly. It's a big thing down here. He got a lot of his rich friends to invest in what turned out to be a Ponzi scheme."

Marcie waited for Sheila to continue, but there was a long pause. Finally she decided to fill the gap.

"I'm sure that's an interesting financial story, but I don't see how it fits in with the *Weird Happenings* column."

"He's dead."

"Kronberg is dead," Marcie said, sitting up straighter in her chair. "When did that happen?"

"Yesterday. He was hiking and fell off a mountain. West Peak, it's right near Meriden."

"Okay, but I still don't see—"

"He saw the black dog," Sheila said in a somber voice.

Marcie stopped for a minute, trying to figure out the significance of that comment.

"I'm sorry. I don't know what that means."

"There's a local legend down here that if you see this mysterious black dog three times while you're on the mountain, you die."

"And did Kronberg see the dog three times?"

"He saw it twice, according to his wife. Of course, we don't know if he saw it three times because he was alone on the mountain when he died."

"You mean he might have see it a third time and that's when he fell off the mountain?"

"Exactly."

"Well, I could do some research on the black dog and then write an account of what happened. It would be good to have his wife's story in her own words. Maybe I could come down for a quick visit and talk to her."

Sheila cleared her throat, indicating that there was something more. "I know from reading your column that sometimes you find that what appeared to be a supernatural event was actually carried out by flesh and blood people. That might be the case here."

"What are you getting at?"

"As you can imagine, Jerome had a lot of enemies in the area after his scheme was revealed. I'm just wondering if someone murdered him and hoped that the black dog would get the blame."

"Would anyone seriously think that?" asked Marcie, tapping her pen on her notebook.

"Some might. More would probably think it was a suicide."

"Are there any people he swindled who would be angry enough to murder him?"

"Several of them are pretty angry."

"Would they be willing to talk with me?"

Sheila laughed. "One thing these people are more than willing to do is talk about what happened to them. They feel aggrieved and want everyone to know what Kronberg has done to them. A lot of these people are my friends, so if I vouch for you, they'll be happy to answer your questions."

"I'll need to get permission from my managing editor, but if she says it's okay, I'll give you a call and set up the trip."

"Great. I'll look forward to meeting you in person."

Marcie hung up the phone and smiled. *Who said the universe wouldn't provide?* she thought to herself; just when things seemed to be heading in the direction of more of the same, a nugget like this was dropped in her lap. A mysterious black dog and unexplained death. A mixture of excitement and fear went through her at the thought of another adventure.

Chapter 3

Amanda's computer screen was filled with the manuscript of an article she was editing, but she was ignoring it, and instead staring out the window at the distant ocean. Marcie stood in the doorway for a moment. Amanda was usually very focused. It was unlike her to be daydreaming in the middle of work, but lately she'd seemed preoccupied. Marcie knocked gently on the door frame. Amanda swung around in her chair as though startled from a deep reverie.

"Hi, Marcie." She smiled and waved her toward the chair in front of the desk.

Marcie took a seat. "Is everything okay?"

"Why do you ask?"

"Just that you seemed to be staring into space."

Amanda shrugged. "I've got a few things on my mind, and to be honest, this article isn't all that fascinating. Another piece about Boston right before the revolution. I'll bet I've read a hundred of them. But our readers seem to like the topic. What can I do for you?"

"I'd like to go out in the field to investigate a story."

"What's it about?"

Amanda's right hand went up to twist the pearls around her neck. Marcie knew that Amanda always got nervous at the thought of her being out in the field all alone. Both of them, however, were aware that given the short staffing, there was no alternative.

Marcie filled her in on the situation that Sheila Little had described.

When Marcie finished, Amanda steepled her fingers and sat back in her chair.

"Sounds promising. I've heard of this Jerome Kronberg, too. I didn't know he'd died."

"It only happened yesterday."

"Are you sure there's enough here for a story? I mean people die in hiking accidents all the time."

"Not after they've seen the black dog twice. You've got to admit that sounds like a genuinely weird happening."

"Could be," Amanda admitted, "especially if his wife backs up the story."

"And I'd also like to follow up on the murder angle. There are lots of people down there who won't be sorry to see him dead."

"So the supernatural is possibly not the criminal."

"Just like most of these cases."

Amanda sighed. "That means you'll be heading into dangerous territory again."

"You know I'll be careful."

"There's something I have to tell you. I've been putting it off because you haven't gone out in the field in quite a while. But after your last adventure, when you ended up almost being killed, Sam made a policy change."

Marcie groaned. Sam Peabody, the older man who was owner of the publishing company that put out the magazine, always seemed to be interfering in what Marcie saw as her right to do her job as she thought fit.

"What is it now? Last time he wanted me to stay in cheap motels to save a few bucks; that's how I almost ended up dead. What brilliant new idea does he have now?"

"He doesn't want you travelling alone. He thinks these investigations are too dangerous for you to take on by yourself."

"Fine. So let him hire a third editor, then you and I can go together."

Amanda shook her head. "That's not going to happen."

"So what then?"

"Sam has found someone to travel with you and help with the investigations."

"Who?"

"A man Sam went to college with."

"You want me to travel with some old guy?"

"He's only in his early sixties. He's not decrepit. He's a college teacher who took early retirement."

"What did he teach?"

"English."

"Oh great; not only do I have to travel with him, but he'll probably want to write the story for me."

"I made it very clear to him that he was just a traveling companion and assistant investigator. You are in charge, and all the writing duties are yours. If you want to take advantage of his expertise, that's up to you."

"Have you met this guy?"

"No. But I had a long conversation with him on the phone. He seems nice. He has a good sense of humor and sounds pretty easygoing. There's no reason why you shouldn't get along fine."

Marcie gave her a skeptical glance.

"What's his name?"

"Simon Bannister."

Marcie grunted. "Sounds like an English teacher."

"Don't judge him before you've met," Amanda said. "And remember, Sam is only doing this for your own protection. He likes your column; it brings in readers. But he also wants you to be safe."

"I guess I don't have much choice. But it's only going to work as long as this Simon person knows that I'm the boss."

"Exactly. He's just a part-time consultant." Amanda studied the calendar on her desk. "When did you want to take this trip?"

"I have a couple of things to finish up here today, and I'll bring some articles to edit on my laptop. So I think I could leave on Monday if that's all right with you."

"That should be fine. I'll give Simon a call to make sure he's available."

Marcie opened her mouth, about to say something about going alone if he wasn't free, but Amanda held up her hand.

"Let's not anticipate problems. Okay."

Marcie nodded, acting more agreeable than she felt, and left the room.

She went back to her office and slumped down in the chair. It wasn't like she usually worked alone. In the first year or so she'd traveled with Amanda. That had been a good partnership. And she'd worked other times with people—generally journalists—that she'd met while in the field. But to be saddled with an English teacher and someone old enough to be her father? Her father. She certainly hoped he wasn't anything like him. That would put a quick end to their relationship.

A few minutes later, Amanda appeared in the doorway and gave her a thumbs up.

"Simon will drive here from where he lives on the North Shore. He'll arrive by nine o'clock on Monday."

"I wanted to leave earlier."

"You have to be reasonable. He has a two-hour drive to get up here. So we can't expect him any earlier than that, can we?"

"No, I guess not," Marcie conceded.

Amanda turned away, then paused and turned back.

"Don't worry. If this set-up really doesn't work out, I'll give Sam a call and tell him that he has to find someone else. I don't care if Simon is an old friend."

Marcie nodded and smiled. "Thanks Amanda; I know I can count on you."

And you'd better get ready to make that call, Marcie said to herself.

Chapter 4

Marcie was sitting in her office on Monday when she heard heavy footsteps on the stairs. At the sound of the creaking floorboards, she looked up and saw a man walking down the hall toward her open office door. He looked to be a bit over six feet tall, solidly built, and bald. She was pleased to see that he was casually dressed in a sweater and slacks rather than wearing a suit and tie. His round face was smiling as he entered her office and stuck out his hand.

"I'll bet you're Marcie Ducasse," he said. "I'm Simon Bannister."

"Yes, I'm Marcie," she said, taking his large hand. His grip was firm but gentle, not an attempt to prove anything, a point in his favor. Marcie was always put off by men who tried to crush your hand to prove their masculinity.

Marcie pulled her coat off its hook behind the door.

"Are you ready to go?" She knew that sounded a bit abrupt, so she tried to soften it. "Do you need to make a rest stop before we head out?"

"I'm all set."

Marcie led the way down the stairs and out into the parking lot.

"Shall we use my car or yours?" Simon asked.

"Mine," Marcie said louder than she intended. She knew that whoever's car was used would probably drive, and she wanted to get this whole thing started correctly, with her in charge.

"Okay." The man went over to a late model sedan and opened the trunk. He took out a suitcase and carried it over to Marcie's hatchback. As he stowed it inside, he glanced at her bag.

"You travel light," he said.

For a girl, Marcie guessed was the implied comment. But she decided not to make anything of it.

"I've been doing this for a while. I've got my own system."

Marcie secured the hatch, and they got in the car. She pulled out of the driveway and headed south on Route 1.

"Have you been up this way before?" Marcie asked when they'd been on the road for a few minutes.

"I've been to Portland and did a little touring in Kennebunkport once, but otherwise no. I tend to go out to the Cape when I want the ocean."

Marcie wondered if that was an implied criticism of Maine, but decided to let it slide.

"Amanda told me that you used to teach college. Where was that?"

"A small place up in Vermont, Ravensmont College. They had to close a couple of years after I left because of finances. But it was a nice school. There were small classes and good colleagues."

"But you retired early."

She thought for a moment that he wasn't going to take the bait and answer.

"There was a good financial package. Plus I saw the handwriting on the wall for the place and knew it was time to bail."

"What do you do now?" Marcie asked.

"Occasionally I do part time teaching at colleges in the Boston area, but basically I'm retired. That's why I agreed when Sam asked if I'd be interested in this job. In fact I've been eagerly waiting for us to have a chance to work together. I've read your column and really enjoyed it."

Marcie glanced over at him to see if he was sincere. He appeared to be, but how could she be sure. Maybe he was only being polite, wanting to keep his job.

"Thank you," she said. Then trying to sound more gracious she added, "Coming from an English professor that really means something. I'll bet you've written a lot yourself."

"Professional articles, that sort of stuff, mostly. I wrote one book."

"What about?"

"*Tristram Shandy*. Have you ever heard of it?"

"Sure, it's a novel by Laurence Sterne. I was an English major in college. I'm pretty sure I read part of it for class."

"Good for you. Most of my students tried to avoid the novel. Too difficult."

"What's the title of your book? Maybe I can get it out of the library some time."

He didn't answer for a moment and when Marcie glanced over he was looking a bit uncomfortable.

"I doubt you'll find it outside of a university library. The title is *A Meta-Critical Analysis of Tristram Shandy.*"

Marcie smiled. "Kind of a mouthful."

"To the handful of scholars interested in the topic, the title said it all. I'm afraid it was never destined to be a best seller."

"Limited audience?"

Simon nodded and blushed slightly. "Let's just say it sold in the hundreds rather than the thousands."

"Popularity isn't always a sign that a book is good," said Marcie.

"I suppose not," Simon said, then he smiled. "All the same, a few more readers would have been nice."

Marcie returned the smile.

"Since you were an English major, were you ever interested in writing a novel?" Simon asked.

"No. I double majored in journalism, and that's where my primary interest lies."

"How does journalism fit in with working at *Roaming New England*?"

Marcie paused for a moment to think. "I guess I consider myself to be an investigative reporter, but instead of probing into politics or corruption, I focus on so-called supernatural events."

"So you don't believe that there really are supernatural events. I was wondering whether you really believed in these so-called phenomena or not. I have to tell you right up front that I'm a doubter, so I'm glad to hear that you are, too."

Marcie shook her head.

"My position is a lot more complicated than that. Sure, I think a lot of supernatural events are really done by humans, but I've seen enough stuff that I can't explain to make me at least keep an open mind about the whole thing."

"Really?"

Marcie nodded. "That's also the best way to approach each case if you want to get a good story. Keep an open mind, and follow the evidence."

"I'll remember that."

Marcie swung off of Route 1 and took the overpass over and down to Route 95. They went along for several miles in silence.

"There's something I wanted to say to you right up front, so that we'll have a good working relationship," Simon began.

"What's that?"

"Well, I know that I'm old enough to be your father, maybe your grandfather, but I wanted you to know that I'm not going to try to take charge. You're the boss here."

"Good, that's the way I see it, too," Marcie said firmly. "And if you don't mind, I'd like to think of you as a colleague rather than a father."

"Yes, a father daughter relationship is a little too close."

"Not in my case."

"You don't get along with your father when you see him?" asked Simon.

"I don't see him," Marcie replied in a tone that discouraged any further questions.

Forty-five minutes later, Marcie got off of 95 and went onto 495 South toward Worcester. Just south of the city, she got on the Massachusetts Turnpike getting off on Route 84. She followed 84 down into Hartford where she navigated the intersecting highways to pick up 91 down to Meriden.

Conversation had been sporadic along the way. When they'd stopped for lunch, Simon had talked a bit about what he liked and didn't like about college teaching.

"Are we going to go into Meriden?" Simon asked as they headed down Route 91.

"No, we're going to swing off north of the city and jog over to catch Route 15. That should bring us right into Comford. That's where Kronberg lived and where our contact, Sheila Little, has her house."

"Where are we staying?"

"In an inn on Route 15 right in Comford. It should be a pretty nice place. Sam is letting us pick better places now because he thinks they're safer."

"Safer or not, I'd rather stay in a nice place," Simon said.

Marcie wondered if he was going to be a difficult traveler, one of those people who never found things to be satisfactory.

Twenty minutes later, they pulled into the parking lot of the Comford Inn. There was a central building with a semi-circular porch extending out toward the parking lot. What looked to be two later additions, by the style of the siding, extended back at a ninety-degree angle from the main building.

Simon gave a low whistle. "Pretty impressive. It's large for an inn."

"Let's hope the service lives up to the looks," said Marcie.

They walked up onto the porch and through the double glass doors into the lobby. On the left was a large desk, behind which stood a young woman in a tailored blouse and black skirt who smiled at them.

"May I help you?" she asked.

Marcie gave her the pertinent information. While waiting for the processing to be complete, she glanced to her right and saw, through large floor to ceiling windows, that there was an indoor pool right off the lobby. The woman noticed the direction of her glance.

"The pool is open until eleven o'clock at night."

"Good. I'll probably take advantage of it. Do you also have an exercise room?"

"Yes, it's down the hall off the pool."

When their registration was completed the woman told them that their rooms were 33 and 34 which were in the north wing. They got in an elevator right off the lobby that took them to the third floor, then began walking in the direction of the sign on the wall that pointed toward the rooms in the thirties.

When they were standing in front of their rooms, Marcie said, "Why don't we take a moment to settle in? I'll give our contact person a call. Since it's only three o'clock, she might be willing to meet with us this afternoon."

Simon nodded. "Sounds fine."

Marcie used her key card to open the door. She went inside and swung her suitcase onto the bed, then dug her cell phone out of the pocket of her jacket and called Sheila Little. The woman sounded happy to hear that they were in town and suggested that they come over as soon as they got a chance. Marcie said they'd be there in half an hour. Then she carefully unpacked her suitcase and arranged things in the large dresser along one wall. She hung her blouses and slacks in the closet. When she was done, she went over to the window and stared outside at the parking lot below. Marcie could feel the excitement rising. It was great to know that the hunt was on.

*****

Amanda Vicker sat at her desk and stared out at the ocean that filled the horizon line. She was finding it difficult to concentrate on the article in front of her. All her mind could focus on was Richard Canton, the man she'd been dating for the last year. She was angry with herself. It wasn't like her to allow her personal life to get in the way of work. She prided herself on being able to compartmentalize things. One compartment held her work and all that entailed, another held her mother and her brothers, and a third one contained the rest of her out of work interests and relationships. This system had functioned well for her since she'd been an adult. But in the time that she'd known

Richard, he'd repeatedly threatened to break out of his box and interfere in the rest of her life.

Amanda had to admit that in a way this was exciting, but it also frightened her. She'd seen too many of her friends travel down the road to heartbreak when they became obsessed with a man who either didn't feel the same way about them and broke off the relationship or who married them and then turned out not to be as compatible as they'd expected. Having a particular man constantly on your mind in the present was no guarantee that he would remain interesting in the long run, Amanda warned herself. People can change over time. Maybe she'd be such a different person in ten years that Richard would no longer love her, even if she continued to love him. Or he could change. The negative possibilities were intimidating. Amanda had to admit to herself that she didn't like to take chances, either professionally or personally. She wondered if that made her some kind of control freak.

She sighed and decided to call it quits early, since she wasn't doing anything productive. Amanda shut down her computer, but remained seated behind her desk. She knew why her relationship with Richard was so much on her mind. It was because she feared that he was as in love with her as she thought she might be with him. He was also taking her out to eat tonight at a very nice restaurant, and the rather solemn look on his face when he told her made her suspect that he was planning to take their relationship to the next level by proposing. If that did happen, how would she respond? She had no idea. Fascination and fear had so far battled to a draw.

Why can't he be happy with things just the way they are? she asked herself. People always want more than they have in the present, and a good part of the time the changes they make just end up costing them what they've already got.

Amanda put on her coat, went to the door and switched off the light. She walked down the hall, pausing briefly outside Marcie's office. She wished she could be more like Marcie, who went long periods of time without a boyfriend and didn't seem to find it disturbing. Whereas she would desperately look for an immediate replacement once a relationship had ended.

Maybe Richard wasn't planning to propose. He could have something completely different on his mind. The resort inn that he managed seemed to fill all of his time when he wasn't with her, and it was frequently their topic of conversation. It could be that he just wanted to inform her of some major renovation that he was planning to undertake. She tried unsuccessfully to convince herself of that, but her instincts told her it was something more.

Am I the only woman who doesn't want her boyfriend to propose to her? Amanda wondered with a grim smile as she opened the door and left the building.

Chapter 5

"What do you know about this Sheila Little?" Simon asked as they pulled out of the inn's parking lot.

"All I know is that she reads our magazine and must have money because she's friends with these people that Kronberg swindled."

Marcie was tempted to tell Simon that Little particularly liked the *Weird Happenings* column, but she thought that might sound too much like tooting her own horn. In her family you never bragged about your accomplishments. You just got the job done and then moved on to the next thing.

"Rich, that should be interesting."

"Rich people give me hives," Marcie said.

Simon looked at her and smiled. "Why is that?"

"Oh, I suppose it's because I think they're looking down on me."

"All rich people have is a lot of money."

"Isn't that enough?"

"Maybe Sheila Little will look up to you because you write an important column in a well known regional magazine."

"Do you think so?" Marcie said in a skeptical tone.

"One thing money can't buy is talent."

"I'll try to keep that in mind."

After a drive of several miles, they found themselves in a neighborhood of large houses set back from the road. Marcie saw the number eleven on one of the two stone posts that framed a driveway, and turned in. They went up a long road to the house, which was made of brick and in the Georgian style. The main house had two attached wings. The one in front of them was a three-car garage, and on the other side of the house was a structure with a lot of windows that appeared to be a solarium. The house wasn't new. It looked like a place built fifty years ago by someone with money.

They parked the car in front of one of the garage doors, and went up a wide sidewalk to the entrance. Marcie pressed the doorbell, and a few minutes later the front door opened wide. Sheila Little isn't little, was Marcie's first thought. She was almost as tall as Simon and had an athletic body that exuded good health.

"You must be Marcie Ducasse," the woman said, sticking out her hand and giving Marcie's arm a good pump. "And you are . . .?"

"This is Simon Bannister," Marcie said. "He's assisting me in the investigation."

Sheila gave his hand the same vigorous treatment while her eyes gave him a thorough once over. Marcie guessed that Sheila was somewhere in her fifties, and wondered if she was on the lookout for a boyfriend.

"Follow me. We'll talk in the plant room. My cleaning lady is doing the den and the living room today."

She began walking briskly down a hall to their right that appeared to run the length of the house. Marcie managed a quick glance into a richly paneled room with walls filled with bookshelves. A woman was in there using a feather duster on the rows of books. After a long walk, they turned left into a room with floor to ceiling windows. Plants in large pots were arranged around the room to create a sitting area in the middle, which was filled with furniture having wrought iron frames and plush cushions. Sheila sat down and gestured to the two chairs across from her.

When everyone was settled, Marcie cleared her throat, took out her notebook and said, "Well, I guess we should start at the beginning. We know what Kronberg did from what we've read in the papers. Is there anything you can add to that?"

"Not really. He was a trusted investment counselor who steered his clients into a fund that he and two other people owned and ran called Three Star Investments. It turned out that there was no investing taking place at all and the entire thing was one big Ponzi scheme that enabled Kronberg and his two partners to get rich."

"And the people who were defrauded lived around here?"

Sheila nodded. "Almost exclusively, and a number of members of the local country club were among them. As you can imagine, when this all came out, Jerry Kronberg wasn't very popular on the links."

"Do you know the people he swindled?"

"A number of them. And probably if you talk to one, he'll give you the names of others. They're a tight group brought together by shared misery. The one who was most angry is Ralph Berenson. He publicly threatened Kronberg, and used to follow him around town, virtually stalking him. Kronberg got a restraining order against him."

"I wonder what the police make out of Kronberg's death?" asked Marcie.

Sheila reached out to pluck a dead leaf from the plant beside her.

"I happen to be friends with the Chief of Police. They're treating it as a suicide."

"Jumping off a mountain seems an odd way to commit suicide. You might just cripple yourself and live," Simon said.

Sheila shook her head. "Not from where Kronberg fell. It's a sheer drop of over a hundred feet to the rocks below."

"Did he leave a note or indicate to anyone that he was planning to commit suicide?" asked Marcie.

"No."

"And what do you think?" Simon asked. "Are you a fan of the mysterious black dog?"

Sheila smiled. "I'm not superstitious, although there have been quite a few people over the years claiming to see the black dog. To my mind, he either jumped or was pushed."

"Which do you think?" asked Marcie.

She shook her head. "I didn't know Jerry well enough. And who really knows how anyone will react when they're under the kind of pressure he was? Being hated by his former friends and facing a prison sentence could cause anyone to snap."

"Losing all your money to a Ponzi scheme could also cause someone to snap and become a murderer," Marcie said.

"The people I know who lost money don't seem like murderers, but, you're right, who knows what a person seriously wronged might do."

"It sounds like this Ralph Berenson was already close to losing it," said Marcie. "Maybe he took it one step further."

"I suppose it's possible. But he's more the type who would get in a shoving match with Jerry and punch him in the nose on impulse, rather than someone who would plan to murder him on top of a mountain."

"Who do you think we should begin by talking to first?" asked Marcie.

"I'd start with Jerry's wife, Yolanda Kronberg. She can give you a good idea of what was going through Jerry's mind right up to the time of his death. Let me give her a call to see what I can set up." Sheila stood up and walked out of the room.

"So what do you think so far?" Simon asked Marcie.

"I think we're lucky to have Sheila. These rich people normally wouldn't give us the time of day. Sheila provides us with access to a world that would otherwise remain closed to us."

"Maybe. Or maybe they'd talk to us anyway because they'd like nothing better than to see their grievances aired in a regional magazine."

Marcie nodded. "And it looks to me as if there are three possibilities for how Kronberg died: he jumped, he was pushed, or in some strange way the black dog caused him to fall."

Simon grinned. "My money is on one of the first two."

"It's too soon for me to tell," Marcie said. That got her a raised eyebrow from Simon.

"You'll have to forgive my manners," Sheila said, walking back into the room. "I was so anxious to talk about the case that I forgot to ask if you'd like something to drink."

Marcie and Simon both declined.

"Well, then, you'll have to join me for dinner tonight."

"We don't want to inconvenience you," Marcie began.

"Nonsense. I'd be delighted to have the company," Sheila said, her eyes lingering for a moment on Simon.

"In that case, thank you," Marcie said.

"I spoke to Yolanda, and she can see you right now. Her house is only ten minutes away." Sheila handed a piece of paper to Simon. "I drew a map from here to her house."

Simon took the map from her hand and thanked her. Marcie glared at him. He gave a helpless shrug as if to say that it wasn't his fault that Sheila thought only a man could read directions.

Sheila escorted them to the front door.

"I hope you get useful information from Yolanda. I look forward to hearing about it tonight." She stared directly at Simon. "Shall we say around seven?"

Simon wisely waited until Marcie said that would be fine before nodding.

"Sorry she seemed so focused on me," Simon said, after giving the first part of the directions to Marcie.

"Not your fault. I think she likes you. By the way, are you single?"

"Divorced."

"That's okay then, we wouldn't want Sheila to be disappointed too soon."

"Are you suggesting that I should lead her on, so she'll keep helping us with the investigation?" Simon asked with a frown.

"I would never suggest that. I'm saying be nice to her, just like you'd be to anyone who was helping us. Can you do that?"

"Sure. I guess I can."

Marcie glanced over at his troubled face and grinned to herself.

"Good," she replied.

Chapter 6

When they got to the end of Sheila's map, they found themselves confronted by a large contemporary house: vast expanses of glass with different roof angles jutted toward the sky.

"This place looks more like a museum than a private home," Simon said.

Marcie pointed to double glass doors placed asymmetrically along the front façade.

"That might be the front door."

They followed a walk that seemed to ramble through several beds of plants and bushes before finally depositing them before the doors. Marcie pressed a button that set off what sounded like a Chinese gong within the house.

A few seconds later, the front door opened to reveal a woman in her midforties. Yolanda Kronberg was slender almost to the point of emaciation. She seemed jumpy, her eyes darting back and forth nervously between Marcie and Simon as they introduced themselves.

"We'd better go into the living room. My brother Charles is here."

They walked down a hallway that was paneled completely in wood with metal decorations hanging on the walls. The ceiling was all glass, giving a panoramic view of the sky. Marcie had seen skylights before, but never one that replaced the whole roof with glass. She wondered how it was kept so clean. They turned left and entered a room where the entire front wall was made of glass. A tall, slender man stood up from an oddly shaped sofa that had a chrome frame and what appeared to be extremely hard cushions.

The man came forward and stuck out his hand.

"I'm Charles Foster, Yolanda's brother and her lawyer."

After the greetings were concluded, Marcie and Simon settled into chairs across from the sofa, where Foster was slumped back comfortably while his sister remained perched on the edge of the cushion.

"What is it that you'd like to know?" Yolanda Kronberg asked.

Her brother held up his hand like a stop sign.

"Before we get into that," he said to Simon, smiling to take away the sting of his interruption, "I'd like to know what you plan to do with anything we might tell you."

Marcie cleared her throat. Reluctantly Foster's glance turned to her. "My intention is to write a story for the *Weird Happenings* column in *Roaming New England Magazine*. It would primarily be about the legend of the black dog, but would also discuss the circumstances leading up to Mr. Kronberg's death in the context of that legend."

"It sounds to me like you want to sensationalize my brother-in-law's death by using it to promote paranormal mumbo jumbo," Foster said. "I'm not sure we have anything to say to you."

"What do you think, Mrs. Kronberg?" Marcie asked, hoping she was more open to being interviewed than her brother.

The woman twisted her hands in her lap and looked down for so long that Marcie thought she wasn't going to answer.

"You're going to look in to the circumstances surrounding his death?" she finally asked.

Marcie nodded. "As much as we can."

"Yolanda—" her brother began.

"No," she said turning towards him. "The police have stopped doing anything. They're convinced that Jerry committed suicide just because they can't figure out what happened. I don't care if these people think there are ghosts around every corner as long as they keep the investigation of Jerry's death alive. I won't have our sons believing their father committed suicide without a whole lot more evidence than I've seen so far."

Charles Foster looked like he was about to say more; instead, he gave a sort of helpless shrug.

Marcie took out a notebook and placed it in her lap.

"Could you tell me how your husband came to climb up West Peak on the day he died?"

"In the last two months or so, climbing West Peak had become something of an obsession for him. Jerry would get so restless just sitting around the house worrying about his legal problems that he had to find a way to escape. Climbing West Peak seemed to provide him with a brief period of relaxation. He would do it every three days. He kept to a regular schedule. I think he liked the structure it gave to his week."

"I'm afraid that I got him started on it. We hiked up the first time together," said Foster. "I never expected him to take to it so much."

"You should have," Yolanda said, giving him a sidelong glance. "You remember when he took up running, how compulsive he became about it, or the time he learned to play bridge. My husband developed passions for things that lasted until he got tired of them."

"When did he start seeing the black dog?" Marcie asked.

"About three weeks ago. It must have been on his third or fourth hike up to the peak," she replied.

"What did he say about it?"

"Just that he'd seen a funny little black dog running around up by the Peak. He wondered how a dog had gotten up there all by itself."

"Did he know about the legend?" Simon asked.

Yolanda shook her head. "Not at first. I told him about it." She looked a bit guilty at even knowing about such a thing. "Some of the women at the club were talking about it one day. That's how I knew."

"How did your husband react to the story?" asked Marcie, looking up briefly from writing down notes.

"He just laughed it off. Jerry wasn't superstitious."

"Did you talk about it with Jerry?" Marcie asked Foster.

Once again Foster's eyes went back to Simon. "I think he did mention it to me in a sort of joking way. Neither one of us took the story seriously. Lots of people hike up to West Peak every year, and nobody gets hurt. There was no reason to believe some silly superstition."

"But didn't Mr. Kronberg see the dog again?" Marcie asked.

Yolanda Kronberg nodded. "About a week later. He saw the dog in the same spot, right near the Peak."

"Did that cause him to take the superstition more seriously?" asked Simon.

"No. He thought that it was just a wild dog that liked to hang around up there. But when Jeffrey Hunter was found dead the same day...."

"What do you mean?" asked Marcie.

"Well, the superstition of the black dog says that nothing bad happens to you the first time you see it. The second time you see the dog something bad happens in your life," Yolanda Kronberg said, twisting her hands together nervously.

"Jeffrey Hunter was one of Jerry's partners," Foster said. "He couldn't take the pressure of the police investigation, so he committed suicide."

"How did he do it?" asked Simon.

"Sat behind the wheel of his car with the motor running in his closed up garage," Foster explained.

"If you believe it was suicide," Yolanda said.

"Is there any reason to doubt it?" Marcie asked.

Yolanda moved even further forward on the cushion. "Of course, there was no note, and Jeffrey never said anything about taking his own life. Plus a number of the people living around here lost money by investing with Jerry and his partners. At least one of them publicly threatened Jerry. And I know that Jeffrey got threatening phone calls just like we did."

"Do you know who was threatening your husband and Hunter?" asked Simon.

"We don't know the identity of the callers, but Ralph Berenson was stalking Jerry. My husband even had to have a restraining order taken out against him. He could have known when Jerry went hiking and followed him up the path and killed him."

Yolanda looked over at her brother for support. He nodded tentatively.

"Have the police looked into whether Berenson could have done it?" asked Simon.

Foster cleared his throat. "The police say Berenson claims to have been home alone at the time."

"That isn't much of an alibi," said Marcie.

"No," Foster continued. "But no one can place him anywhere near West Peak at the time of Jerry's death either."

"He was there or somebody just like him. Some lunatic who wanted to blame Jerry for everything," Yolanda said.

"And you have no idea of the identity of the callers who threatened your husband?" Marcie asked.

She shook her head. "Some of them were hang ups, but most of the time the person would say something like 'you're dead' or 'why do you go on living?' I heard several of them myself until Jerry got our number changed and unlisted. It wasn't always the same voice. Who knows how many people were planning to get revenge?"

"I guess it's understandable that people would be angry," Marcie ventured.

Yolanda Kronberg leaned so far forward on the couch that Marcie thought she was going to leap at her.

"But they shouldn't blame Jerry. He was just the front man who went around convincing people to invest. He believed it was a good investment. He was as duped as his clients were. The whole scheme was developed by his partners. Jerry was a good man; he wouldn't have purposely tried to cheat his friends."

Marcie nodded, wondering how much of this was a wife's love allowing her to deceive herself.

"Who were his partners other than this Jeffrey Hunter?" asked Simon.

"There was only one other, Stanley Wilkie."

"You said that Hunter committed suicide. I assume Wilkie is still alive?" Simon asked.

"He's alive," Yolanda said, "but he doesn't leave the house or answer his phone. I'm not even sure that he'll open his front door. But he doesn't know anything about Jerry's death. The people you should talk to are the ones who were angry with Jerry because they were duped."

"People like Berenson?" Marcie asked.

"And others. Ask around at the country club. You'll get lots of names."

"We'll do that," said Marcie starting to rise. Then she paused as she thought of another question. "Did your husband take the black dog legend more seriously after the death of his partner? After all, it would seem like the story was coming true."

"He was shaken by Jeffery's death," Yolanda said, "but that's only natural. They'd been friends for several years. He did skip his hiking up the mountain for several days. Perhaps the superstition was on his mind, but then I think he decided to defy his fears. His last words to me were, 'It's bad enough that I may have to go to jail. I'm not going to imprison myself out of fear.'"

Tears began to run down her cheeks and she wiped at them with a tissue.

Foster stood. "I'll see you out."

"Thank you for your help," Marcie said to the woman as she and Simon arose.

Mrs. Kronberg nodded her head. "Find out what really happened to my husband."

"We'll try," Marcie said.

Charles Foster led them to the front door. He opened the door and stepped outside, motioning for them to follow him.

"I don't want Yolanda to hear this," he said softly. "But Jerry was very anxious about the likelihood of his going to prison. I think it's a very real possibility that he committed suicide.

Yolanda will never believe that, but I'm afraid it's true."

"Did he discuss suicide with you?" asked Simon.

"Not directly. But I knew Jerry quite well, and I could tell he'd reached the end of his tether. As the prosecutor built a stronger and stronger case, Jerry became more and more depressed. Hunter's suicide may have put the idea into his mind."

"What about the possibility of murder?" asked Marcie.

Foster waved his hand dismissively. "Making anonymous phone calls and shouting insults is about the level of threat these folks pose. This is the country club set, not a bunch of gang bangers. Words are their weapons of choice. Plus most of them still have plenty of money left to lead a very comfortable life. They wouldn't want to risk going to prison. Don't mention it to Yolanda because she doesn't know, but even I lost a bit of money by investing with Jerry. I was pretty angry at first, and Jerry and I had a nasty argument, but our rift had pretty much healed over by the time of his death."

"What about your sister's view that Jerry didn't know the investment was a scam?" asked Marcie.

"Jerry knew. He had to. He didn't invest in Three Star himself, so he didn't lose any money when the whole thing fell apart. It's natural for Yolanda to want to see him as a gullible victim, but I'm afraid it just won't wash."

Marcie and Simon thanked Foster and headed to their car. When they were out on the road back toward their inn, Simon turned to Marcie.

"So do you think Foster has this right, and Kronberg committed suicide?"

"I might be more convinced if it weren't for the black dog."

"You think the black dog caused him to fall off the mountain?" Simon asked, not able to keep the skepticism completely out of his voice.

"I don't know. But two appearances of the black dog seem like more than a coincidence. I think somebody was planning for Kronberg to fall off of that mountain."

"Assuming that's the case, where should we start?"

"I think we take Yolanda's advice and begin with the angry investors, starting with the angriest of them all: Ralph Berenson."

"If he'll talk to us."

"He'll talk to us. He's a man with a grievance and wants the world to hear about it. And it's likely that Sheila knows him and can vouch for us."

Simon nodded but didn't say anything.

"You don't think this is the way to go?" asked Marcie.

Simon pulled the seat belt away from his neck and let it snap back in place.

"I don't know. But I can understand why a man like Kronberg would commit suicide rather than go to jail. I might do the same thing. Jail is a hard place to adjust to for a normally decent person."

"You may be right, but I think we have to eliminate the possibility of murder first."

Simon nodded. "I can see that."

Marcie remained quiet for a moment, then she said, "Did you notice the way Foster ignored me and only talked to you?"

"I guess it didn't register with me, and I don't think I encouraged him."

Marcie thought back to their conversation. Simon had sat there quite impassively, and had only asked a few questions. She couldn't blame him for Foster's behavior.

"You didn't. It wasn't your fault."

Simon remained silent for a moment, then he said, "You know, this is going to happen sometimes when we're together. People tend to assume that the older man is automatically the one in charge. I'm not sure there's much we can do about it."

"I don't think there is, and it's not a problem as long as *we're* clear on who's in charge."

"I'm clear," Simon said with a smile.

Marcie smiled back. "So am I."

Chapter 7

When they got back to the inn, they went to their respective rooms after agreeing to meet in two hour's time to go to Sheila Little's for dinner. Marcie changed into her swimsuit. She stopped off at the main desk for a towel, then went into the pool area. No one was around, which was the way she liked it. You couldn't really swim laps in a crowded pool. She started swimming in a leisurely crawl, then slowly got into the rhythm and could feel her mind begin to relax. Back and fourth she went, up and down the length of the pool. As she focused more and more on her breathing, she found that the concerns of the day dissolved into nothing, leaving her feeling relaxed but more alert.

After twenty minutes she climbed out of the pool, dried herself, and sat in one of the plastic patio chairs that were arranged around the edge. Gradually her mind returned to the issues of the day. Marcie found herself doubting Charles Foster's conclusion that none of the people that Kronberg had defrauded would be capable of murder. Just because a person had money and belonged to a country club didn't mean that he wouldn't resort to violence for the sake of revenge. In fact, from Marcie's limited knowledge of the rich, based on a few friends in college, rich people often paid more attention than most to what happened to their money. And being taken advantage of by a so-called friend would probably make them vindictive.

What about the possibility of suicide? Marcie didn't think it could be ruled out. After all, Jerry was facing the very good possibility of prison time. He had also lost most of his friends and the respect of his community. But she found herself siding with Yolanda Kronberg. Her husband showed concern for his situation—who wouldn't?—but he didn't seem abnormally depressed. He was out hiking several times a week, and his last words to her about not letting fear rule his life seemed to indicate that he did not see his future as hopeless.

There was also the question of Jeffrey Hunter's death. Apparently the police saw that as a suicide. Marcie wondered if there was some way she could find out more about it. She decided to bring it up with Sheila in the evening. Maybe her contacts in the police department could be helpful. If there was a chance that Hunter had been murdered, that would make it more likely that someone was systematically killing the investment partners.

Of course it was always possible that Kronberg had died as a result of seeing the black dog three times, Marcie thought, standing up and walking out of the pool room. She'd seen enough strange occurrences in her relatively brief time at *Roaming New England* that she couldn't reject a paranormal explanation out of hand. But she wasn't going to go in that direction without a lot more proof.

*****

Two hours later Marcie and Simon were heading over to Sheila Little's house.

Marcie had just laid out her thinking to Simon to get his reaction.

"Well I certainly agree that the supernatural explanation should be our last resort," Simon said. "Although I'll admit that seeing the black dog twice is quite a coincidence. I think I'm a little more inclined to go along with Foster and favor the suicide explanation. Like I said before, the thought of imprisonment at this point in his life would have been a serious shock to someone like Kronberg. Plus he had the example of his partner's suicide to put the idea in his head."

"But would he commit suicide by jumping off a cliff?"

Simon shrugged. "It's hard to put yourself in the mind of someone who's suicidal. Maybe being on the top of that mountain was where he felt most free. It could be that each climb up the mountain was a way of preparing himself for the final act."

"It still strikes me as an odd method."

"If we're talking about odd, it's also an odd way to murder someone."

Marcie smiled. "You're right. Every possible explanation of Kronberg's death sounds pretty unlikely. Maybe if we get more information things will come into a sharper focus."

They parked in Sheila's driveway. After they rang the bell, Sheila Little quickly opened the door. Marcie noted that her eyes once again gave Simon a careful onceover. Marcie had to admit that he did look rather distinguished in his tweed jacket with a carefully knotted tie beneath a buttoned-down collar.

Sheila led them down the same hall they'd been in that morning, but she took a left turn before they reached the sunroom. They were in a large dark green room, the center of which was dominated by a long table.

"I hope you don't mind if we get right to the eating," Sheila said. "We're going to skip the cocktails. But if you'd like some wine with dinner just say so. My late husband laid in an extensive wine cellar. I've pretty much given up alcohol, too many empty calories."

Simon and Marcie both indicated they would follow her example.

A woman wearing a chef's jacket appeared from a door at the back of the room carrying a tray that she put down on a server in the corner of the room. She gave each of them a salad, which after a couple of bites Marcie thought was the best salad she'd ever eaten. She said as much to Sheila.

"Yes. Isn't Susan wonderful? She's my personal chef. Not that she's mine alone. She works for several people in Comford. Most nights I just heat up a meal that she's prepared for me and left in the refrigerator, but when I have guests, she's happy to come by and serve."

"It's a wonderful luxury," Simon said.

"Actually, for me it's a necessity. I cooked when my husband was alive, but after he died, I found myself eating only processed food and high fat desserts. My weight skyrocketed, and my doctor warned me that my cholesterol was getting dangerously high. I knew that I'd never be able to keep to a healthy diet if I did my own cooking, so I got in touch with Susan. She comes in the morning and makes my lunch and dinner. Now I have tasty, wholesome meals."

An hour later Marcie had to admit that she had consumed one of the best meals in her life. Everything was wonderful, from the salad through the chicken, which tasted different from any chicken she'd ever eaten. They had large helpings of fresh vegetables, and ended with what seemed to be a decadent chocolate mousse, although Sheila reassured them that it was lower in calories than they might think. When Sheila asked if they'd enjoyed the meal, Marcie eagerly nodded her head in appreciation, while Simon became positively poetic.

"Good, I'm glad you liked it. Now it's time to get down to business."

Sheila had led the conversation over dinner into a discussion of books, movies, and her terrible golf game. Marcie sensed that she didn't want to talk about Jerry Kronberg in front of Susan. She'd also managed in a fairly subtle way to discover that Simon was divorced.

Sheila led them back down the hall to the room filled with books that Marcie had noticed in the morning. Sheila indicated that they should occupy the three chairs clustered in front of the fireplace.

"This was my husband's study," she said waving a hand around the room at the walls filled with books. "He really didn't like to read, at least not anything other than stock analyses and reports of corporate earnings. He had a book dealer come in and fill the shelves with the sort of books a person with a study should have. He thought that it would give his business associates the impression that he was a deep thinker. Poor Harold was always trying to compensate for the fact that he never went to college. He came from a modest background and was a self-made man. Even though he was shrewder that most of those he did business with, he could never quite get over a feeling of intellectual inferiority."

"A formal education might give you a certain type of knowledge, but being smart is something you're either born with or not," said Simon.

Sheila nodded and allowed her gaze to linger on Simon a bit longer than necessary. "Too bad you didn't know Harold. Maybe you'd have been able to change his view of himself."

"Did Harold know Jerry Kronberg?" Marcie asked.

"Sure. Harold was very active in the country club. He was on the governing board. So he knew Jerry and most of the people he defrauded."

"Did you invest any money with Jerry?" asked Marcie.

"Not a penny," Sheila replied. "Harold died before Jerry's scheme really took off, but he was always suspicious of Kronberg. He couldn't understand how Kronberg could be paying a rate of return that was so much higher than the market. He said it was obvious that something slippery was going on."

"Why didn't the others see it?" Simon asked.

"They were blinded by greed. As Harold always said, if something seems to be too good to be true, it probably is."

"Yolanda Kronberg told us that the police are closing out her husband's case as a suicide. Do you know if that's accurate?" asked Marcie.

"The police Chief and I are old friends, and that's what he told me, too," said Sheila. "They figure things got to be too much for him and he jumped."

"But there was no note," said Marcie.

"I said the same thing to the Chief. He told me that not every suicide leaves a note. He figures that Jerry did it more on impulse. He'd been climbing up there day after day thinking about it all the time, until finally he found one day that he'd worked up the courage to do it."

"Yolanda thinks he was murdered," Simon said.

Sheila pursed her lips. "No one wants to think that a loved one committed suicide. If she believed that, she'd have to admit to herself that Jerry didn't confide his feelings to her or that he did and she didn't help him. Either way she'd come to believe that she'd failed him as a wife. Yolanda doesn't want to do that. What woman would?"

"That's pretty much the analysis given by her brother, Charles," said Simon

"Oh, was Charles Foster there? I guess he'd want to be there to look after Yolanda's interests. He's a very good lawyer. He's handled several real estate transactions for me, and he drew up my last will."

"Was he involved in representing his brother-in-law in any way?"

"No, he doesn't do criminal law. And he had nothing to do with Jerry's business."

"But Yolanda could be right about his being murdered. There actually were people who hated him," Marcie said, pulling out her notebook. "What about this Ralph Berenson guy? He sounds like he was over the top."

"Ralph followed Jerry around calling him names and telling anyone who would listen what a sleaze Jerry was. But the restraining order put an end to that."

"Was there ever any physical threat?" Marcie asked.

"One time Jerry approached Berenson, trying to explain things, I suppose, and Ralph pushed him away. That's what really led to the restraining order."

"So you don't think that Berenson was the kind of guy where angry words lead to action?"

"Ralph has always been someone who gets easily excited, and he does tend to take things personally. But I never thought of him as dangerous; he's more a Chihuahua than a pit bull."

"Would it be possible for us to speak with him ourselves?" Marcie asked.

Sheila stood up. "Let me go find out. I'll give him a call."

After she left the room, Marcie turned to Simon.

"I think we should try to interview several of the people who lost money because of Kronberg."

Simon looked doubtful.

"Why not?" Marcie asked.

"I'm sure the police have interviewed all of them, and they haven't found out anything."

"Maybe the police didn't try very hard if they assumed it was a suicide."

"Okay, that's possible. But remember, the black dog is what your story is going to be about. How do we link Kronberg's possible murder with his seeing the black dog twice?"

Marcie frowned. She was still frowning when Sheila reentered the room,

"Well, it's all set. You can talk to Ralph Berenson at his home tomorrow morning at nine o'clock." She handed Marcie a sheet of paper. "I sketched out a map from your inn to Berenson's house. It's not very far; nothing is in Comford."

"Thank you for setting it up," Marcie said.

Sheila studied Marcie's face. "What's the matter? You look unhappy."

"Simon just pointed out to me that the black dog is really the topic of our story. And I'm not sure how that fits in with the possibility of Jerry being murdered. It seems to me that we have three possibilities: Jerry committed suicide;

someone pushed him off the cliff; he saw the black dog for the third time and in some way fell to his death as a result of that."

"There's another possibility," said Simon. "It could be that the murderer used the black dog as a way of frightening Jerry so he'd be easier to push off the cliff."

"The murderer would have been taking a risk that after the first sighting Jerry would be so frightened that he would stop hiking up to West Peak," Sheila said.

"He might have known how determined Kronberg could be," Simon said. "According to his wife he was given to becoming obsessive about things. Once he started climbing, he kept doing it on a regular schedule."

"I guess we'll just have to start by interviewing some of the people hurt by Kronberg," Marcie said.

"If you need a go-between to set up any more interviews, let me know. I'd be happy to help," Sheila said, giving Simon a radiant smile.

"That's very kind of you," Marcie said, trying to keep a smile off her own face. "I just had one more question."

"What's that?"

"Do you know any of the details of Jeffrey Hunter's death?"

"I know that the police saw it as a suicide by carbon monoxide poisoning."

"Was there anything unusual about it?"

Sheila stared across the room for a moment. "The only thing odd was that he had a high level of sleeping pills in his system."

"Isn't that strange?" asked Marcie.

"Not according to the Chief. He told me that lots of suicides take drugs or alcohol to ease their way into killing themselves. So he wasn't particularly surprised that Jeffrey had drugs in his system."

"Were you surprised to hear that Hunter had committed suicide?"

"Actually, I was, because of the three of them, he seemed to be the mentally toughest of the group. He was a surgeon and well respected around town. But I guess you can never tell about someone."

"Thank you for all your help," Marcie said.

"My pleasure," Sheila replied, looking at Simon.

Chapter 8

Amanda sat across the table from Richard and tried to eat. She knew that the lamb on her plate tasted wonderful, but her mouth was so dry she could hardly swallow. Even the normal movements of eating with a knife and fork felt awkward to her, as if she was so totally caught up in the fear of what Richard was going to do that she couldn't spare any energy for the regular functions of life.

Richard was talking. It was a good thing he was so animated because he'd had to carry more than his share of the conversational load this evening. She tuned back in to what he was saying, and was relieved to find that he was still discussing his plans for expanding the resort inn. This was a topic that so frequently came up between them, she could respond appropriately while on mental autopilot. Maybe this was the important topic that had motivated Richard to take her to this fancy restaurant, she thought hopefully. She kept nodding and mechanically eating until they were finally done, and the waiter whisked away their plates.

Amanda had just managed to convince herself that it was safe to relax and enjoy the evening, when Richard stopped talking and looked at her with frightening intensity. The napkin she was using fell from her hand and floated to the floor. She left it there and told herself to focus on what Richard was saying.

"We've been going together for almost a year now," Richard said. "And I don't know about you, but it's been the happiest year of my life."

Amanda forced herself to nod her head. Whether it was true or not, she wasn't sure, but normal politeness made her agree.

"I feel that it's time for us to increase our commitment to each other," Richard said standing up.

Amanda hoped, against all logic, that he was on his way to the men's room, but instead he took a step toward her and in a graceful motion dropped to one knee. A ring box materialized from a jacket pocket. He opened it, and she saw a stone reflecting the light from the candle on the table around the room. She became conscious that the people eating at the nearby tables had paused in their conversations and were watching them expectantly.

"Amanda," he said in a solemn voice, "would you do me the honor of becoming my wife?"

There was what seemed to Amanda like a long silence as she tried to decide what to say. She almost said, "I don't know." But that seemed terribly indecisive, and she felt an overwhelming pressure not to disappoint Richard or the people at the neighboring tables.

She gave a short jerky nod, which she was sure appeared more like a spasm than an affirmation. Richard must have thought so, too, because he continued staring up at her with his earnest brown eyes. She had always loved the expressiveness of his eyes, and she couldn't bear to see them filled with hurt and disappointment.

"Yes, I will," she said in almost a whisper.

Richard smiled, his face a combination of happiness and relief. The people at the neighboring tables clapped and offered their congratulations. Richard took the ring from the box and slid it on her finger, where it fit perfectly.

"I told the jeweler that I didn't know if you would like the ring, and he said that we can exchange it if you preferred another. We'll have to take it in to get it fitted, anyway."

"It's fine," she said.

Amanda looked down at the diamond glittering on her finger. It felt strange seeing it there, a brilliant sign that something important had changed in her life.

"It's fine," she repeated dully.

Richard began talking about wedding plans. Amanda struggled to follow along. He wanted to have the reception in the banquet room of his inn. He thought they might as well save their money for the purchase of a house. Amanda nodded her head, still dazed. And when Richard pressed her for a more specific answer on some things involving the wedding, she asked for some time to think about it.

When she had begged off making a decision for about the tenth time in a row, Richard smiled.

"I realize that this is quite a surprise for you. I'm sure you knew it was coming soon, but you probably didn't expect it this evening. Why don't we wait for a few days until we get used to the idea of being engaged before we work out the specifics of the wedding plans?"

"That sound like a good idea," Amanda said, relieved.

They skipped dessert but had coffee. They didn't talk much, and Richard spent most of the time looking at her adoringly over the rim of his cup until she hastily gulped down the hot coffee and suggested they leave.

Amanda had been back home for an hour, an hour that she had spent sitting in her rocking chair and trying to come to terms with what had happened. At first she'd been angry at Richard for popping the question in a public place where she could hardly give a negative answer without embarrassment. However, she knew that even if it had been just the two of them in her living room, she would have found it difficult to refuse him face-to-face. Why couldn't he have asked by e-mail, she thought, then I would have been able to put him off with a vague answer. I'm much better with the written word. She smiled to herself at the idea of such an impersonal way of proposing.

The phone rang. It was Marcie, and she immediately launched into a detailed description of her day. She talked about the issue of whether Jerry's death was a suicide, a murder, or a paranormal happening. Finally, she noticed that Amanda was barely replying.

"What's been happening up there with you?" Marcie asked.

"It looks like I'm going to get married," Amanda replied.

"*It looks like*," Marcie said. "It can look like snow or look like the economy is going to tank. Those are predictions. When it comes to a marriage, you should know whether you said 'yes' or 'no.'"

"I said 'yes,' at least sort of."

Marcie was stunned. Amanda was always the cool rational one, and suddenly she was sounding like a ditzy high school girl.

"What do you mean, 'sort of'?"

Amanda explained how the proposal had come about and her mixed feelings.

"You've been going out with Richard for a long while. Haven't you ever thought about whether you love him enough to marry him?"

"Whenever I've thought about it, I've pushed the idea away. It was something I figured I'd focus on some other time. I think I love Richard, but I don't know if I can trust anyone enough to commit to spending my life with him. I don't want to make a bet that I'll always feel the same way about him. People change. How can I be sure that the love will last?"

"You can't. It's always a gamble. Some of the biggest rewards in life only come about if you're willing to take a risk."

"I suppose," Amanda said.

"Why don't you get some sleep. Things will probably seem better in the morning."

"I certainly hope so."

When Marcie hung up the phone, she sat on the bed staring across the room and thinking about the advice she'd given Amanda. She'd spent all day hearing about people who'd trusted someone and suffered a major financial loss as a result. How could you know when to trust and when to be cautious? Maybe the best you can do, Marcie thought, is to be diligent in making your decision and then go ahead without looking back. Not a perfect answer, she admitted, but nobody ever said that life was perfect.

Chapter 9

"The food here is really good," Marcie said, digging into her stack of blueberry pancakes.

Simon nibbled on his roll and smiled. "If I ate that way I'd blow up like a balloon."

"So would I if I didn't exercise. I went out for a three mile run this morning."

Simon gave an exaggerated sigh. "Folks like you set an incredibly high standard for the rest of us."

"Once you make exercise part of your daily schedule, it's easy to do," she said primly.

"I suppose. Although I still think it takes a lot of discipline."

"Well, it's particularly important to exercise when you're on the road because you eat more than you would at home. Although I guess that's not true of everyone," she said, eyeing Simon's half eaten roll.

"Do you travel a lot?" Simon asked.

"Occasionally, but it's just regional travel. The only longer trip I've taken lately was last fall to a conference of magazine editors and writers in Las Vegas. What about yourself?"

"I used to travel to scholarly conferences around the country and even in Europe back when I was working. I've pretty much given all of that up. But I do go to San Francisco and Seattle a couple of times a year. My children live out there."

"They're grown up?"

Simon nodded. "My son is twenty-eight and my daughter is twenty-three."

"I guess you get along pretty well with them if you visit so often."

"I get along a lot better with them now that I did when they were teenagers."

"Teenagers can be difficult," Marcie said, remembering her own teenage years.

"Well, all the normal rebellion of those years was compounded by the fact that they were in high school when their mom and I split up. For a long time they blamed me because I was the one who filed for divorce."

Marcie nodded. Not comfortable asking personal questions, she focused on her breakfast.

"Their mother and I had what people today would call a toxic relationship. We were much worse together than we were apart." Simon stopped and gazed across the room. "My wife is a sculptor. We met when I went to one of her exhibits at a local art studio. I always admired her creativity. When the kids came along, she had less and less time for her work. I helped out as much as I could with the child rearing, but still a lot of it fell to her and she came to resent it."

"That must have changed as your children got older."

"Yes. And she went back to her sculpting. She worked hard at it and produced lots of pieces, but couldn't seem to get anything shown in a larger venue than local art shows. My wife is very ambitious, and her lack of success made her bitter. She blamed her failure on not having been able to actively pursue her art for so many years. She made it sound as if the decision to have a family was all mine, and that I didn't do my share in taking care of the children. Neither of which is true."

"It's hard to be reasonable when you suffer a big disappointment."

"And I understood her feelings. I was able to develop my career during all those years when she was primarily looking after the children. So it must have seemed to her that I sucked out the best years of her life and left her unable to create. I understood her, but it became impossible for me to live with her. We did nothing but bicker and argue all the time. It wasn't healthy for us or the children."

"But your kids didn't understand that."

"For them I was the one who broke up the family. And the family they knew was better than having no family at all. But as time went by I think they began to appreciate why I did what I did. So we have a pretty good relationship now. I even get along somewhat better with my wife. Her sculpture finally has started to sell, so she's feeling more positive about life in general."

"Nobody said relationships were easy," Marcie said, knowing she sounded trite.

"Do you have a boyfriend?"

Marcie shook her head. "Not right now. The last guy I went out with lived too far away for us to keep things going. How about you, any woman friends?"

"Not at the moment."

"I know somebody who might be able to fill that slot."

"You mean Sheila."

"She seems to have taken a liking to you."

"She certainly is full of energy."

"And apparently has lots of money."

"That's what worries me."

"Aren't you the one who told me only yesterday that money was nothing compared with talent?"

Simon smiled ruefully. "Unfortunately that sounds familiar. But I was talking about a professional relationship; it's different when you start dating. I think Sheila is rather out of my league."

"She seems like a pretty regular person to me. I'm not sure money matters to her all that much, and you'd certainly be a change from her husband who never read a book."

"Now you've got us married. Aren't you hurrying our relationship along a bit?"

Marcie shrugged, ate the last piece of pancake then looked at her watch. "I guess we'd better hurry if we want to be on time for our meeting with Ralph Berenson."

"Just the way I like to start the day, interviewing a crazed stalker."

"If he is crazed, then he probably has nothing to do with Kronberg's death," Marcie said.

"Why do you say that?"

"Because if Kronberg was murdered, whoever did it was far from crazy."

* * * * *

"Turn left at the next corner," Simon said

Marcie turned the wheel and pulled onto a tree-lined street. The houses were perhaps fifty years old. The yards nicely landscaped. It was definitely a good neighborhood, but not filled with palatial homes like Sheila Little's. They drove two blocks with Simon staring at the facades trying to discern the numbers.

"Here we are," he said suddenly.

Marcie pulled the car over to the curb in front of a two-story brick house. They got out of the car and started up the walk. They were only halfway to the house when the door opened and a thin, nervous looking man came out on the porch. He stood there shifting his weight from foot to foot. In his arms he carried a small brown and white terrier that kept stretching its neck toward the visitors as if hoping to break free and greet them before its master. Man and dog gave the impression of pent up energy.

"I assume you are Marcie Ducasse and Simon Bannister?" the man said as they reached the bottom of the stairs.

After they said that they were, the man pushed the door open with his shoulder to allow them to enter.

"I have to put Rebecca in her cage or else she'll be jumping all over you. She gets excited at seeing strangers."

From the jerkiness of the man's movements and the way his head bobbed up and down as if agreeing to unspoken statements, Marcie decided that Rebecca wasn't the only creature in the house that was easily excited. As they went down the hall, Berenson gestured with his free hand toward the living room and said that he'd be right back. Marcie settled into the sofa and Simon sat in an armchair off to the side. The room was sparsely furnished, as if there had once been more furniture that had mysteriously disappeared piece by piece. Berenson came into the room and perched on a chair across from Marcie.

"So I understand that you're writing a story about how Kronberg defrauded his best friends," Berenson said, his hands becoming claw-like, as if he wished he could get them around Kronberg's throat to kill him for a second time.

Marcie explained that they were primarily interested in Kronberg's death. She said nothing about the black dog, figuring that Berenson would think they were crazy sensationalists and refuse to talk to them.

"I think it's obvious that he jumped off that cliff, taking the coward's way out, which would fit him perfectly."

"So you don't think it's possible that's someone murdered him?" asked Marcie.

Berenson shrugged. "I don't know all the people he defrauded. Maybe he invested money for some criminals who couldn't wait for the wheels of justice to sort things out. But I don't think any of the folks in Comford would murder him."

"You were pretty angry at him," Simon said, smiling to defuse the question.

"Of course I was," the man said sharply. Then he paused. "Look. I didn't always live like this. I used to have a wife and family. About three years ago my wife suddenly tells me she wants a divorce, and she and my two sons move out. By the time it's all over, she has half of my possessions, and is happily living life on her own. Then I lose my job due to cutbacks in the sale of commercial real estate in

Manhattan. So I figure that I should invest what I've saved with Kronberg to build up my nest egg. That way I can meet my child support payments and have enough to live on until the economy turns around."

"And you lost all that money?" Marcie asked.

He nodded. "My lawyer told me that eventually, after a trial, I might get some of it back. Probably be lucky if it's a dime on a dollar. So I have to go to court to get my alimony and child support restructured. How do you think I feel depriving my boys of the kind of life they deserve? But I didn't have any choice. What little savings I have left I need to live on myself."

"So you decided to follow Kronberg around town calling him names?" Simon asked.

Berenson's mouth pulled back in a gaping grin that Marcie found unnerving.

"You should have seen that guy when I walked into his favorite restaurant when he was having dinner, and pointed him out as the filthy thief he was. You've never seen a guy who wished he was dead as much as Kronberg did at that moment. Every time I exposed him in a public place he got a little smaller and a lot less arrogant." Berenson sat back in the chair and seemed to relax for the first time. "That's why you're wrong if you think that I killed him. I was looking forward to all the publicity a trial would bring. Death is quick; the kind of public humiliation he was confronting would be a slow torture."

"Maybe someone else that he defrauded wouldn't see it that way," Marcie said.

He shook his head. "Like I told you, as far as I know the people he cheated aren't the type who kill. If he'd showed up in the club again, someone might have popped him in the nose. But as soon as he saw blood, the noble avenger would be apologizing and calling for an ambulance."

"Wealthy people might not want to get their hands dirty, but they could hire someone with fewer scruples to do it," Simon said.

Berenson paused as if giving the idea some thought.

"It's possible. But I don't think a hired killer would throw him off a cliff. A bullet to the head or the heart would seem to be the method of choice."

"But then it wouldn't look like suicide," Marcie said.

"Which is probably just what it was," Berenson said.

"Have you heard the story of the black dog?" she asked.

"Almost everyone around here is aware of the story. I heard through the victims' grapevine that Kronberg had seen the dog twice. Third time is supposedly the charm. I don't believe in silly superstitions, but in this case I might make an exception. I would've liked to have been there when he saw that dog for the third time. But like I said, I didn't want him dead; I wanted him to spend a lot of time in prison after a long and highly publicized trial."

"'Victims' grapevine'?" Marcie asked.

Berenson gave another of his unnerving grins.

"Yeah, a bunch of us who were swindled by Kronberg talk to each other regularly by phone, e-mail, or in person. That way everyone stays up to date on what's happening with the case. After I got the call from Sheila last night, I phoned a few others to let them know you were in town. And each of them called a couple of others. You get the idea."

Marcie felt a twinge of anxiety at the thought of having her every move broadcast throughout the community. This could easily create a conspiracy of lies that would prevent her from getting at the truth.

"Kronberg's two partners: Jeffrey Hunter and Stanley Wilkie. Did you hate them as much as you did Kronberg?" Marcie asked.

"In theory we did, but in reality we hated Kronberg more. Sure, they were all in on the swindle, but Hunter and Wilkie just played supporting roles. It was Kronberg who was in charge of marketing. He was the one who looked us straight in the eye and lied about what he was selling us. Plus he was active in the country club; he'd even been membership chair at one time, Hunter wasn't a member and Wilkie hardly ever came to events. That's what made Kronberg's actions more of a betrayal."

"Is there anyone else we can talk to who would help to give us a balanced insight into Jerry Kronberg's personality?" Simon asked.

Berenson stared at the carpet for a moment, then he smiled.

"I can't think of anyone who liked Kronberg much after what he did, but there is one guy at the club, Arnie Getz. He didn't lose as much as most of the rest of us, so he's less angry. He can probably give you a more moderate view of Kronberg."

Berenson took a cell phone from a holder on his waist and scrolled thorough a list of numbers, then he recited one.

"Thanks for your time," Marcie said, writing it down then getting to her feet.

"No problem. Kronberg is one of my favorite topics of conversation. A little like poking at an aching tooth, it makes you feel worse but you can't resist it."

"Maybe you'd be happier if you moved on," Simon suggested.

Berenson's mouth tightened. "I'll move on when I get some of my money back."

Marcie and Simon left the house and were headed down the walk to Marcie's car when Simon asked, "Do you believe him?"

"About what?"

"That he'll move on when he gets some restitution."

Marcie nodded. "Sure, why wouldn't that make him feel better?"

"Because he's really angry at himself. He probably considers himself to be a smart man, so it's humiliating for him to think that he was scammed. That's the sort of thing that happens to other people, to people who're unsophisticated or stupid. He can't forgive Kronberg for showing him up like that."

"So do you think that he had anything to do with Kronberg's death?"

Simon shook his head. "I think he was telling the truth when he said that he was looking forward to seeing Jerry go on trial. That was the only way he'd be humiliated in the same way Berenson was."

"What about one of the other investors as the killer?"

"I agree with Berenson. Unless Kronberg took money from the mob, it probably wasn't an investor who killed him. These country club guys might be into white-collar crime, but they aren't likely to become murderers. Or do you think differently?"

Marcie didn't say anything until they'd gotten in the car and started off down the street.

"Maybe the violence is just a little deeper below the surface among the country club set. Plus this whole thing with the black dog makes me think that someone wanted Kronberg's death to look either like a suicide or some kind of supernatural event. That isn't the way a mobster would go about things."

"So you think it was one of Jerry's former friends?"

"Seems like it to me."

"Berenson's dog was brown and white. Maybe we should have asked if he had a black one around somewhere."

Marcie nodded. "Find the dog and you find the killer. That's a thought."

Chapter 10

The Comford Country Club was a large rambling stone structure at the intersection of two main county roads. Marcie pulled into the first open slots she came to, figuring that on a sunny spring day the golf course was probably busy. She and Simon went through the front door into a large, dark wood-paneled vestibule. From one of the shadowy corners a man wearing a tie and jacket appeared.

"Can I help you?" he asked, politely but firmly.

"We're supposed to meet Arnold Getz," Marcie said.

The man looked at Simon and smiled. The glance he gave to Marcie was more doubtful.

"He may still be out on the course. I'll check in the lounge."

He disappeared into the darkness.

"This place is pretty posh," said Marcie, "but I guess most country clubs are."

"I wouldn't know, I've never belonged to one."

"You don't play golf?"

"I do play, but at a public course. The fees for a place like this are probably a killer."

"Do you play any other sports?"

"I ski and bike a little. Otherwise I go to a health club once in a while, probably not often enough."

"Good for you," Marcie said. She gave him a long once over and decided that he looked in pretty good shape for his age.

Marcie jumped as the man who'd greeted them suddenly reappeared at her side.

"Mr. Getz is in the lounge. If you'll follow me."

They trailed him into a dark corner where large double doors soon became visible. The room he led them into had leather chairs set up in conversational groupings. He went through that room to one that had an ornate bar at one end and tables and chairs arranged around the room. Their guide led them to a table where a man was sitting by a large picture window that framed a beautiful image of the greens, then he silently slipped away.

The man at the table stood.

"Hi, I'm Arnie Getz," he announced, putting out his hand.

He was a large man, as tall as Simon but much heavier. Marcie thought he looked as if he'd once been a football player but over the years his chest had slid down to his waist, a redistribution that even his nicely made suit couldn't conceal. When he gave Marcie's hand a shake, she caught a glimpse of a large complicated watch on his thick wrist. The kind that made Marcie wonder if you could actually use it to tell time.

"Can I get you something to drink?" he offered. He had a beverage in front of him that appeared to be at least primarily orange juice. Marcie and Simon both declined.

"I managed to get nine holes in this morning. I have to slip them in when I can because work interferes." He smiled. "I try not to let work get completely in the way of golf."

"What kind of work do you do?" asked Marcie.

"I'm a tax lawyer." He took a sip of his drink. "Not the most exciting job around, I admit. But I seem to have a knack for it, and it pays the bills."

"Do you think being a lawyer is why you didn't lose as much money to Kronberg as some of the others?" Marcie asked.

Getz sat back and folded his hand across his stomach as if to show he wasn't ashamed of his girth.

"Berenson told you that, did he? You're probably right. Being a tax lawyer probably makes me a bit more prudent than most. But I did give Jerry some money to invest, partly because he was getting these fantastic rates of return. And even more because I liked Jerry, though I never completely bought into his spiel. It sounded too good to be true. But everybody else was doing it, so—"

"You invested with him in order to fit in with the crowd?" asked Simon.

Getz took a sip of his drink and gazed benignly around the room.

"We all know each other here. I wouldn't say we're all friends, but we're close enough that we share business tips. And there's something of a herd mentality. When a good idea comes along a lot of the members get on board, especially when the tip is coming from someone who seems to be doing very well. It also didn't hurt that Jerry was popular with almost everyone here. He had a gift for making friends."

"Had he been a member of the club for long?" asked Simon.

"Only for about four years."

"And did he have this same investment company for all that time?"

Getz shook his head. "About three years ago, Jerry, Jeffry Hunter and Stan Wilkie set up this investment firm. Three Star Investments, they called it. Right out of the gate they started making great profits, and word got around. So when Jerry started talking it up among the members, he quickly had a waiting list of potential investors."

"And you were on that list, but you didn't invest as much?" said Marcie.

Getz gave a low chuckle. "Just like when I go to Vegas, I never take more than I'm comfortable losing. But a lot of guys put almost their entire nest egg in Jerry's basket, so when the bottom fell out, they were devastated."

"Like Berenson?" Marcie said.

"Exactly. But at least he had the excuse of being in the midst of a messy divorce that clouded his judgment. Most of the other investors were just greedy. They saw this as a quick way to big profits."

"What caused the scheme to unravel?" Marcie asked.

"What usually happens with Ponzi schemes. You have to keep taking in enough new money to pay off the earlier investors. Well, the economy took a downturn, people stopped investing, and at the same time, some others wanted to pull their money out. Jerry and his partners just didn't have the cash available to pay people off. Some folks complained, and before long there was a federal investigation." Getz sighed and patted his stomach, "Lots of people refused to believe that Jerry could have been so duplicitous even when the overwhelming evidence started to come out."

"But fortunately for you, you'd been cautious."

"Still he had virtually stolen fifty thousand of my money, so I wasn't thrilled. But it wasn't more than I could afford to lose."

Getz took a sip of his drink and studied the tablecloth for a moment.

"There was another reason why I was cautious."

"What's that?" Marcie asked.

He shrugged his heavy shoulders. "I shouldn't really call it a reason, it was more an intuition. Anyway, I was never convinced that Jerry and his partners were smart enough to successfully run an investment firm. Jerry had some kind of a background as an investment banker, but whenever I tried to discuss the market with him, he put me off. I came to wonder if he actually knew what he was doing. His partners were even less impressive. Wilkie is a lawyer, who has lots of family money but to my knowledge never actually practiced any profession. Hunter was a medical doctor. I didn't know either of them well, but they didn't strike me as highly skilled investors."

"Why do you think Kronberg needed partners in the first place?" asked Simon.

"Jerry had to have some initial seed money, so he could pay out dividends from the beginning. Wilkie is wealthy. He also needed local credibility. Hunter is well respected in the community. Add in Jerry's sales skills, and before long people were begging to give him their money."

Getz was silent for a few moments. The only sound was the tapping of his finger against the now empty glass.

"The thing is," he said finally, "not only wasn't I impressed with them as legitimate investors, but since the scandal came to light, I've never really thought the three of them were smart enough to come up with such a good Ponzi scheme. They sent out phony quarterly reports that looked convincing to a lot of guys who really knew something about investing. Ever since the story broke, I've been wondering if there wasn't a fourth partner, a silent partner, who was really the brains behind the whole thing. Somebody who didn't want his name to be known if the whole scam went south."

"Any candidate for the position?" asked Simon.

Getz shook his head.

"Some people seem to think that Jerry committed suicide. What's your opinion?" asked Marcie.

The man frowned. "Jerry generally seemed like an upbeat guy, but who knows what someone will do if he's facing serious jail time? I never thought that Hunter would kill himself either. If they hired good lawyers, they could probably make some kind of a deal with the government. It seemed way too soon for them to give up hope."

"Kronberg's wife believes he was murdered," Marcie said.

"I've heard she's been saying that. I think it's pretty unlikely. A lot of people around here might not have shed any tears when they heard Jerry was dead, but most of us were pretty shocked. I don't think anyone around the club was angry enough to kill him."

Getz checked his complicated watch. Marcie saw that he apparently could tell the time with it because he stirred restively.

"He'd seen the black dog twice on top of West Peak," Marcie said quickly before the man could leave.

Getz smiled. "Now that would be an amazing story if Jerry saw the dog a third time then fell."

"Don't you think it's pretty amazing that he even saw it twice?"

"I suppose, if it were true."

"Why would Kronberg lie about it?"

The big man shook his head. "I wouldn't say he lied. But maybe the suicide theory is right, and he was starting to lose it. The dog could have been a figment of his troubled mind."

"Can you think of anyone who might have been messing with him?" asked Marcie.

"You mean someone spooking him with a black dog? I can't think of anyone. But I've only been on the periphery of this whole thing, and there are lots of people in Comford who were swindled that I don't know about."

"Who would know?" Marcie asked.

Getz stared across the room for a moment as if trying to decide whether to help them or not. He finally picked up his cell phone that was on the table next to his drink.

"Florence Lee has been the sort of unofficial organizer of all the victims here at the club." He ran through a menu on his phone then read out a number to Marcie, who copied it down in her notebook.

"She should be able to tell you, if anyone can, whether someone was trying to frighten Jerry," Getz said standing up. "I have to go off to work now if there's nothing more."

"Do you own a dog?" Marcie asked.

Getz smiled. "You mean a black dog? My wife has a cat. That's the only pet in the house."

"Thanks for your time," Marcie said.

"No problem." He paused for a moment. "You know there's someone else you might want to talk to and that would be Stan Wilkie."

"The remaining partner," said Simon.

"He might know whether someone was trying to put the fear of God into Jerry. Who knows, someone might have been doing the same thing to him. The only problem is that Stan has become a virtual recluse since the scandal broke. But I'm sure you reporters have a way of getting to people."

"I'm sure we do," Marcie said with more confidence than she felt.

Chapter 11

"Hang on a second," Marcie said as she and Simon walked through the vestibule of the club.

The man who'd escorted them in was standing by the front door. Marcie asked him if he had a local phone book. He went over to a bookcase hidden in the darkness of a corner and returned with one. Marcie quickly looked through it, then returned it to him with thanks.

Getz was right," Marcie said as they walked across the parking lot. "Wilkie's number is unlisted."

"Not surprising. If he'd had a listed number, he was probably getting a lot of hate calls."

"I'd still like to talk with him. Getz is right, Jerry might have told Wilkie if they were in any danger."

"Why don't you call this Florence Lee? If she's as involved in organizing the victims as Getz believes, she might have Wilkie's number."

Marcie took out her notebook and punched the number into her cell phone. When a woman answered who identified herself as the housekeeper, Marcie asked to speak with her employer. A firm voice came on the line and asked her to state her business. Marcie explained that they were writing a story about the Kronberg fraud and wanted to have the victim's point of view. After a long pause, the woman agreed to meet with them in the early afternoon. Marcie wrote down her address and a set of directions.

She put her notebook away and turned to Simon.

"We have a couple of hours. Why don't we go back to the inn and have lunch?"

"Are you hungry again?" Simon asked with something close to amazement in his voice.

Marcie grinned. "I never miss an opportunity to eat."

*****

"This sandwich is really good," Marcie said, opening her mouth wide to take another bite.

Simon nodded and speared another couple of leaves from his salad.

"Are you on a diet or something?" Marcie asked.

"Or something," Simon said looking forlorn. "My doctor says my cholesterol is too high, and that if I don't lower it by dieting, I'll have to go on medicine. And I hate medicine, especially the kind you have to take for the rest of your life."

"But if it makes you better—"

Simon held up his hand. "Don't take this the wrong way, but I think this is one of those things that you have to be older to understand."

Marcie took another bite of her sandwich and focused on chewing, a good way to avoid saying something she'd later regret. After she swallowed, she decided to change the subject.

"It's really a shame that Kronberg's sons are left without a father. I wonder how the family will do. Yolanda didn't strike me as a take charge person."

"People who seem weak sometimes rise to the challenge. When my wife and I split up, I was afraid that she was going to collapse. But she didn't; she held it together, and made a good home for our kids."

"But you weren't dead."

"I may as well have been for the first couple of years. My wife had the kids turned against me to the point that they never wanted to have me visit or come to my apartment."

"But later things changed, and you got back together. Your kids had the option to do that, Kronberg's boys won't have that choice. It's important to have a father."

"True. But you suddenly seem to be giving a rather exalted role to fatherhood, considering that you don't have a close relationship with your own father."

"Some men aren't cut out to be fathers. But you strike me as good father material and for all we know, Kronberg, despite his faults, might have been as well."

"What exactly made your father so unfit?"

"His personality."

"Could you be more specific?"

Marcie sighed. "Let's just say that he was career military and always treated me as if I was one of his more disappointing recruits. His idea of punishment was to lock me in a closet for a night if I broke curfew."

"Sounds cruel."

"To be fair, I don't think he looked at it that way. He thought I'd never get on in life without the discipline to adhere to rules. Discipline is the one thing I learned from him, and I have to admit that it has proved helpful."

"People always have excuses for the bad things they do."

Marcie nodded. "He went too far, and that was wrong. But I don't think he was ever honest enough with himself to realize that."

Marcie finished the last of her sandwich, and Simon pushed what remained of his salad to one side.

"Aren't you going to finish that?" asked Marcie.

Simon shook his head. "And don't tell me how there are people starving in the world, so I shouldn't waste food."

"I wouldn't dream of it. I don't believe in guilt-tripping people into doing what they don't want to do."

"Good. Shall we go to see Florence Lee?"

"Sure. And if you get faint with hunger in the middle of the afternoon, we can stop somewhere. I can always eat."

Simon smiled. "I'll keep that in mind."

*****

The woman who answered the door and introduced herself as Florence Lee appeared trim and fit in her jeans and sweatshirt. She had a stylishly cut helmet of white hair. Her face suggested that she was in her late fifties, but she could have been older. The overall impression she gave was of someone who could be forceful to the point of unyielding. She ushered them into a room to the right of the doorway. It was painted a dark moss green and contained a sofa and a couple of chairs in a formal arrangement that suggested the room was rarely used except as a place to talk with people who were not close friends.

When they were all seated, Florence said immediately, "I really hate discussing this."

"I imagine it must be very painful," Marcie said gently.

"What's painful about it is that it makes me feel like a foolish old woman. A foolish old woman who allowed herself to be flimflammed by Jerry Kronberg into making a sizeable investment in a fraudulent scheme."

"Did you seek him out or did he come to you?" asked Simon.

"He came to me. I was one of the first people with whom he discussed the Three Star investment. And heaven help me, I was flattered to be among the first to be asked. Jerry had the gift of making you feel like you were the only person in the world who mattered to him. After a few minutes you wanted to do anything you could to make him happy."

"Why do you think he came to you early on?" asked Marcie.

The woman gave a crooked smile. "Because I have something of a reputation around the club of being a shrewd investor. Jerry probably figured that if he got me on board a number of others would follow. He was right. That's what makes me feel the worst; in addition to losing my own money, I was partially responsible for other people losing theirs. People trusted me to be diligent, and I let myself be suckered by a cheap con artist."

"Hardly a cheap one," Simon said. "He seems to have been very skilled. He fooled a lot of smart people other than yourself."

She nodded. "Thank you for trying to make me feel better. I know you're right, but I can't keep from blaming myself for letting greed and smooth talk cloud my judgment. I've tried to make it up to the others by organizing an informal group of folks who were cheated."

"What does the group do?" Marcie asked.

"Mostly we share information about the legal status of our claims, and we urge the prosecutor's office to keep investigating."

"How does Jerry's death affect that?"

"Well, it brings the criminal case against him to a conclusion, but there are still charges pending against Stanley Wilkie and Three Star itself. Also the civil suit against the investment company and the three partners will go forward, and much of the evidence discovered in the criminal case will be helpful in that."

"Were you surprised when you heard that Jeffrey Hunter had committed suicide?"

"Certainly. But no more surprised that I was by the fact that he was involved in this Ponzi scheme in the first place. He was a highly respected surgeon in the region. No one ever thought he'd be part of anything shady. I suppose that the shame of it all finally got to him."

"Has anything come out to suggest why he became Jerry's partner?"

"I have a friend in the prosecutor's office who says that Hunter liked to gamble and owed a lot of money. That might explain why he went in with Jerry; he needed money to cover his debts."

"What about Stanley Wilkie? Why do you think he got involved?"'

Florence shook her head. "Stan is a puzzle. He's already very wealthy. The only thing I can figure is that he's the kind of wealthy person—and there are lots of them—who can never have enough money. Plus, Jerry probably did as good a job of selling his scam to his partners as he did selling his securities to the rest of us."

"So you think that Kronberg was the brains behind the whole thing?" asked Marcie.

"That's what the prosecutor's office thought, and most of those who lost money feel the same way."

"Arnie Getz seems to think there might be a fourth man involved. He doesn't think Jerry and his partners were bright enough to run such a successful scam."

"Nobody has heard of anyone else being a part of this. But I will admit that I've had my suspicions that all the parties to this scam haven't been revealed."

"Why do you think that?"

The woman paused as if not certain whether to answer or not. Finally she said, "I have a friend in the prosecutor's office who tells me that an examination of the e-mails among the partners of Three Star sometimes seem to allude to a fourth person. It's a matter of interpretation, and the prosecutor's office doesn't seem inclined to pursue it. But I've been pushing them hard to look into it. I've also tried to encourage Wilkie to turn states' evidence and reveal the name of the fourth man, if there is one."

"Do you think you'll succeed in getting him to talk?"

"I'm hopeful, but it's too soon to tell. Maybe as he gets closer to his trial date he'll become more willing to reveal what he knows."

"Do you think Kronberg committed suicide?" asked Marcie.

"You told me over the phone that you're primarily interested in Jerry's death, but I don't know how I can help you. I was surprised when I heard about it, but Jerry was facing a difficult situation. He might have seen suicide as the only way out."

"Did you know that he saw the black dog when he was climbing West Peak?" asked Marcie.

Florence Lee smiled. "I heard about that. He wouldn't be the only person to think they'd seen the black dog."

"Did the others die in a fall from the mountain?" asked Marcie.

"Not in recent times. There are some legends of that happening. I've climbed up there lots of times myself and never seen the dog, so I wouldn't put much faith in the tale."

"Yolanda Kronberg thinks that her husband was murdered," said Simon.

"There are a lot of angry and upset people around here, that's for sure. You've already talked to Ralph Berenson, so you know that. He's acted on his feelings more than others, but that doesn't mean there aren't some out there who've toyed with the idea of getting revenge. If there are, however, I haven't heard about it. Everyone seemed satisfied with the idea that the Three Star partners were going to end up in jail, and we'd get some percentage of our money back."

"You don't think it's strange that two of the partners have already died?"

"As I said, Hunter valued his reputation. Losing that may have made him suicidal. And Jerry might have snapped under the threat of imprisonment. I know all the folks in my organization pretty well, and none of them seem inclined to commit murder. Even Ralph is more talk than action. I think Yolanda would rather see her husband as a victim than a suicide. I can understand that, but I see no reason to believe it to be true."

Marcie glanced at Simon, who gave a small shake of his head indicating he had no further questions. She was about to stand when another thought occurred to her.

"Is there anyone that we can talk to who knew Jerry Kronberg very well, and might be able to give us a good idea of his state of mind?"

"Well, normally I would say that no one knows a man better than his wife, but in this case I'm not sure. From what contact I had with Jerry, I've gotten the impression that he didn't discuss business with her much at all. It was a very traditional family structure: she took care of the home and children, and Jerry worked to support them. That could be another reason for thinking his death was a suicide. When his con was revealed, his ability to provide for his family disappeared, and that could have seriously threatened his concept of himself.

"Was there anyone other than his wife that he might have confided in?" asked Marcie.

"As far as I know, his best friend was Harry Schmidt. If anyone would know Jerry's thoughts towards the end, it would be Harry. I believe that he and Jerry continued to speak to each other even after the scam was revealed."

"Did Schmidt invest any money in Three Star?"

"No, I've heard that he wanted to but Jerry wouldn't let him. I think that was the only instance when Jerry actually tried to prevent someone from being defrauded. In fact some people thought they were so close that Harry must have know what was happening. I doubt that. Harry has always struck me as a real straight shooter, so I don't think he would hide knowledge of a criminal action."

"Do you have a phone number where he can be reached?"

The woman nodded. "It's on my computer."

"And we'd also like to get in touch with Stan Wilkie."

"I have his number as well, but he screens his calls and rarely answers. Let me print them out for you, I'll be right back."

When she left the room, Simon leaned toward Marcie and said softly, "I sure wouldn't want her coming after me. She'd find whatever there is to be found."

Marcie nodded. "If there's another partner involved in this, I think she'll ferret him out."

A few moments later, Florence Lee returned to the room. She held out a sheet of paper to Marcie.

"I printed out Stan and Harry's phone numbers and addresses."

Marcie thanked her, and the woman escorted them to the front door.

"I'd appreciate it," she said as they stood in the doorway, "if you'd inform me of anything you find out relevant to Jerry's scam. The more evidence I have, the more I can pass on to the prosecutor to make sure they are diligent in pursuing this case."

Marcie said that they'd do that. As they walked to the car, Simon asked, "Are you really going to tell her what we find out?"

"Sure, if we learn something new about the fraud. But when it comes to Kronberg's death, we'll keep that information to ourselves unless we have to tell the police."

"Do you really think we're going to make some progress on this?"

Marcie gave him an encouraging smile. "We've just started to pull at the loose threads in this case. Who knows what might unravel?"

Chapter 12

Simon checked his watch as they pulled into the inn parking lot.

"It's three o'clock. Do we have anything scheduled between now and dinner?"

Marcie shook her head. "I'm going to make a couple of calls to see what I can set up for tomorrow. I also brought along some articles on my computer that I promised Amanda that I'd read while I was away."

"Then I think that I'll avail myself of the hot tub they have down in the pool area. It might loosen up some of my stiff muscles."

"They also have a fitness room you could use. A few miles on the treadmill might help those muscles more."

Simon made a face.

"How about we get together in the lobby around six?" Marcie suggested. "Do you want to eat in the restaurant right here?"

"Sounds fine."

Once she was in her room, Marcie took out her cell phone and began calling the numbers on the sheet of paper given to her by Florence Lee. Wilkie's phone rang and rang, but no one picked up. Marcie decided that a visit to his house might be the only way to get in touch with him. Fortunately, Florence had included the address. When she called Harry Schmidt, he picked up almost immediately. Marcie explained why she wanted to see him.

"You're really interested in getting a balanced picture of Jerry?" the man asked doubtfully.

"Of course," Marcie replied.

"It's just that I have no interest in giving interviews that will simply add to the negative publicity surrounding his name. He's gone now, and I think his family should be allowed some privacy."

"I understand. We aren't actually very interested in the Three Stars' case itself. We're more interested in Jerry's death, how it came about and why."

"I'm not sure I can help you much on that. All I know about the event is what I've read in the papers."

"We're primarily interested in gaining information about Mr. Kronberg's state of mind at the time of his death."

"Well, I guess I can help you with that. I saw Jerry the day before he died."

Marcie quickly arranged to meet with Schmidt the next morning at nine-thirty. After she ended the call, Marcie pulled out her laptop and began editing one of the articles she'd brought with her. It was about making maple syrup in Vermont in the nineteenth century. Marcie was surprised to find that maple syrup making had changed little at all in the last hundred and fifty years. When she was finished, Marcie sat staring across the room, letting her mind sift through all that she'd learned in the last day or so.

She could write the story now, given what she knew. It would tell about a man who perpetrated a devious con, and then died on West Peak after seeing the black dog twice and perhaps three times. The story would leave open whether the black dog was to blame for Kronberg's death or whether it came about in some other way. That would be an adequate story, one that was suggestive of the supernatural without making a commitment either way.

Marcie sighed. It was an adequate story, but one she could have written without leaving the office. What she needed was more evidence as to who might have murdered Jerry Kronberg. Marcie had a feeling that if she could discover the identity of the killer, she'd also be able to reveal more about the black dog. As she tried to come up with new avenues to investigate, slowly her eyes closed and she fell asleep. When she woke up almost an hour later, she just had time to change her clothes and get ready for dinner.

"There are so many things on this menu that look good to me, I'm not sure what to order," said Marcie. They were seated at a table by a window that presented a view over an expansive green lawn that ended in a shadowy grove of trees.

"Speaking of meals, Sheila has invited us for lunch tomorrow."

Marcie put down her menu and looked hard at Simon.

"She called you instead of me?"

Simon nervously ran a hand over his bald head as if smoothing down invisible hair.

"I don't think it had anything to do with who is in charge of this investigation."

"What then?"

"I think Sheila really wanted me to come alone. But I pretended to misunderstand her and said we'd both be there at one o'clock."

Marcie relaxed. "You could have gone by yourself. I don't want to stand in the way of true love."

"I don't want to mix business and pleasure. How do we know that Sheila isn't more mixed up in all of this than we think?"

"I doubt that she'd have invited us down here to investigate if she was guilty of any wrongdoing."

"I suppose."

"I think that you're afraid of her because she's such a forceful woman."

Simon frowned. "I wouldn't use the word 'afraid' exactly."

"How about 'scared,' 'frightened,' or 'fearful'? Do I have to go on?"

"Maybe you're right," Simon said with a grin. "Between her money and her personality, I do feel a bit overwhelmed."

"She strikes me as an interesting person. Not getting to know her could be a missed opportunity."

Simon didn't answer. His gaze was fixed at a point somewhere behind Marcie. She twisted around and saw a man of around her own age coming across the room to their table. He had blond hair and was good looking. He was weaving slightly and walking with the focused intensity Marcie associated with someone who'd had too much to drink.

"Do you know him?" Simon asked in a stage whisper.

Marcie shook her head as the man came to a halt in front of her.

"Is this seat taken?" the man asked thickly, nodding at one of the empty chairs at the table for four.

"No," Marcie replied.

After a moment spent struggling to pull the chair out, he sat down on it heavily and stared at the tablecloth as if he'd forgotten what he wanted to say. Finally he looked up at Marcie and frowned.

"I've been told that the two of you are going to write an article about Jerry Kronberg, the sleaze."

"That's right," Marcie said.

The man nodded his head with a sage expression as if some elaborate hypothesis had been confirmed.

"Are you going to try to make him look good? Because if you're going to do that, I must make an objection."

"We're only trying to find out the circumstances surrounding his death," Marcie answered.

"The man deserved to die."

"What sort of a relationship did you have with Kronberg?" asked Simon.

The man squinted across the table at Simon as if he'd just noticed his presence.

"What sort of relationship? What sort of relationship does the sheep have with the wolf?"

"So you invested some money of yours with Kronberg?" Marcie asked.

"Not of mine. That's the problem." The man stopped talking and his chin went down on his chest. Marcie was afraid for a moment that he had fallen asleep.

Suddenly his head popped up. "My respect, that's what he stole from me—my respect."

"What's your name?" Marcie asked.

A puzzled expression crossed his face, then he smiled and extended a hand in Marcie's approximate direction.

"Steven Pawling, at your service." The smile on his face disappeared. "But you're on his side."

"Not at all," Marcie said. "We're just trying to find out the truth."

"The truth is that Kronberg was a sleaze, a lousy sleaze."

"Because he lost your money?"

"Not my money to lose. And he didn't lose it, he stole it," Pawling said loudly.

"Whose money was it?" Marcie asked in a gentle voice.

"Not mine. The family's."

"You invested your family's money with Jerry Kronberg?"

"The sleaze."

Suddenly another man appeared behind Pawling. Marcie recognized him as Charles Foster, Kronberg's brother-in-law.

"We have to go back to our table now, Steven. It's time to order our meals," Foster said with the artificial good cheer that many people use when talking to someone who's drunk.

"Not hungry. I'm trying to explain to this attractive young woman that she has to show that Kronberg was really a sleaze."

"And I told you that we're going to write nothing but the truth," Marcie said.

"We should go back to our table now and let these people enjoy their dinner," Foster said, putting a hand on Pawling's shoulder. Pawling shrugged off the hand and slowly rose to his feet.

Foster put a hand on his arm trying to guide him from the table, but Pawling pulled away. He stood there gazing down solemnly on Marcie.

"I'm going to go now. But promise me that you'll tell the truth about Kronberg."

"I promise."

"Let's go, Steven," Foster said, taking a grip on his arm. Again Pawling pulled away.

"Have to go to the men's room," he announced. His eyes roamed around the room.

Foster pointed toward the lobby. "It's down that hall to the right."

Pawling's eyes brightened. "Then that's where I'm going." Without further comment he began a meandering journey across the room.

"I apologize for Steven's intrusion. I'm afraid that I pointed you out and told him why you were here. But that was several drinks back, and I never expected that he'd come over here while I was in the men's room." Foster paused then said, "May I sit down for a moment."

Marcie gestured for him to take a seat.

"Am I to understand that Steven in some way lost his family's money by joining in Jerry's Ponzi scheme?" Marcie asked.

"Sorry, Steven is my client, so I can't tell you anything about his situation."

"Fair enough," Marcie said.

"I realize it might seem unfair of me to ask since I refused to answer your question, but how is your investigation going so far?"

"We've been talking to various people who've been swindled. There are a number of folks who are very angry with the men who ran Three Star," Marcie said.

"But like I told you at my sister's, there's a huge gap between being angry and deciding to murder someone."

Marcie shrugged as if she wasn't so sure.

"Jerry even scammed me," said Foster, "and I was pretty angry myself. But I didn't want to kill him."

"We also talked to Florence Lee. She mentioned the possibility of there being a fourth partner in Three Star. Someone who wanted to keep his involvement secret."

"No one else has come to light and the investigation is almost concluded. If there was a fourth investor, Jerry never mentioned him to me or to anyone else that I know of."

Foster got to his feet, looking in the direction of the lobby.

"I'd better go check on Steven. The main bar is right near the men's room, he may have gotten sidetracked." Giving Marcie and Simon a small wave, he headed off on the trail of Pawling.

"What do you make of Pawling?" Simon asked.

"I'm not sure. I'd have to meet him when he's sober to decide for myself whether he's capable of committing murder."

"So many people fell victim to Kronberg's scheme that we'll never be able to eliminate all the suspects."

Marcie nodded. "Yes. We can't spend months here interviewing people. I have us scheduled to meet with Harry Schmidt, Jerry's good friend, tomorrow at nine-thirty. I'm hoping that he can give us some idea as to whether Kronberg is likely to have committed suicide."

"Maybe he can also give us the names of the people who hated Kronberg the most?"

"Especially anyone who owns a black dog."

"You really think this black dog is important?"

"I'm hoping it is because it's the only solid piece of evidence we've got."

*****

Amanda sat across the table watching Richard intently. Apparently, this was sort of a business dinner. They were in a secluded corner of the restaurant in the inn Richard managed, but it wasn't a romantic evening. Before they'd gotten their salads, he had a pad of paper open beside his plate and was ready to take notes.

"I thought that we'd set the date for sometime towards the end of October. The tourist crowds are pretty much gone by then, but the weather is still beautiful." He looked up at her expectantly.

"October of this year?" she asked, feeling a tightness develop in her chest.

Richard gave a short laugh. "Of course. We've been going out together for quite a while. I don't think we need a long engagement. Do you?"

Amanda paused, trying to pick her way through the minefield of wrong things to say.

"I think I just need a little while to get accustomed to the idea of getting married," she said hesitantly.

Richard smiled. "I know what you mean. It's a big step. Sometimes I can't imagine that I'm really going to do it. But I'm sure we're just having normal jitters at the prospect of making such a big change in our lives."

Amanda looked into his eyes and saw so much love and devotion there that she wished she felt more certain about her decision. But she suspected her reservations went much deeper than Richard's.

"When I called my folks last night with the news, they were thrilled. I think they really like you."

"I only met them once, that time we had dinner together."

"But we had plenty of opportunity to talk. I think they were impressed by what a responsible position you have, and I think they could also tell that you care about me."

Amanda gave a weak smile. "I like your parents as well. But you know that my parents didn't have exactly a successful marriage, so I'm nervous about rushing into things."

"We wouldn't be rushing. There's more than six months between now and the end of October. Although I wouldn't expect anything to happen during that time that will change our minds, would you?"

"No, of course not. It's just that everything is happening so fast."

Richard reached across the table and took her left hand in both of his. His thumbs rested lightly on the engagement ring.

"Look, since we're having the reception right here, we don't have to worry about making reservations. I'll keep the date open unofficially. We can take a few weeks to think about when we want to do the deed. How would you feel about that?"

"That would be much better," Amanda said quickly, grasping at anything that would postpone the event.

Richard nodded, then leaned across the table to kiss her lightly on the lips. Then he sat back down and picked up his pen.

"But why don't we make a few tentative plans so we have an idea of how many are coming, and where we'll put the people who are staying overnight."

Amanda sighed deeply. "Okay," she said with a thin smile.

Chapter 13

Marcie was awake by six o'clock the next morning. She pulled back the heavy drape that concealed the double window in the bedroom. A sliver of sun was already making its way over the horizon. It looked like a great morning for a run. Marcie quickly changed into her exercise outfit. Down in the lobby she gave a cheerful good morning to the woman behind the desk, then trotted across the parking lot.

The street that ran past the inn had no sidewalks, but it did have a fairly wide grassy shoulder that fell off into a steep drainage ditch running along the length of the road. Marcie turned right and crossed the street, so she'd be facing the traffic. She checked her watch, planning to run twenty minutes out before returning. Within a block or so she got into her rhythm and could feel her muscles beginning to stretch and loosen. After another hundred yards she'd go on autopilot and think of other things.

She began to focus on the questions she wanted to ask Harry Schmidt. As a close friend of Jerry Kronberg, he'd be in a good position to tell whether Jerry was likely to have committed suicide. He'd also know better than most if any serious threats had been made against Jerry's life. Marcie found her mind drifting to Steven Pawling and their meeting last night. She wondered if someone as unbalanced and angry as Pawling seemed to be could have proven a threat to Kronberg.

Marcie looked up and saw a car coming down the road toward her. She made sure she was on the outside of the shoulder in order to give it plenty of room. When the car was a hundred feet away, the wheels suddenly turned towards her, and it came up on the shoulder of the road heading directly at her. She had the vague impression of a hooded figure behind the wheel before she flung herself to her left, lost her footing and rolled down into the drainage ditch. She could feel the breeze of the car as it passed by her.

For a long minute she lay in the bottom of the ditch, afraid to move, and waiting for her heart, which was beating loud enough to echo in her ears, to return to normal. Slowly she unfolded and took inventory of her body. Her legs seemed fine. She stood up and walked a few feet. Nothing seemed to be twisted or sprained. The worst damage was to her forearms and hands which had broken her fall into the drainage ditch and gotten scraped on the stones at the bottom.

She crawled out of the ditch, looking carefully each way to see if the car was waiting for her. No one was in sight. Right in front of her was a sign with an icon warning people to drive carefully because there might be children at play. Marcie crossed the street and ran the quarter mile back to the inn. She slowed down and ran close to the edge of the shoulder every time she saw a car coming, just in case it was her attacker returning. She didn't feel safe until she walked into the lobby. Even back in her room, her hands were still shaking and she felt slightly sick to her stomach. A hot shower helped and she sprayed some antiseptic on her various scratches, so by the time she met Simon in the lobby, she felt back to normal. She must not have looked that way, however, because the first thing that Simon did was ask what was wrong.

Forcing herself to talk slowly and to the point, she explained what had happened.

"I think we should call the police," he said when she was through.

"What good will that do? I didn't get the license plate or even a look at whoever was behind the wheel. There really isn't much for the police to go on. They'll probably just think that I wandered out into the road, almost got clipped, and now I'm hysterically blaming the driver of the car."

Simon took his cell phone out of his pocket. "We'll make sure that they take you seriously."

"Who are you calling?"

"Sheila. I'm sure she'll be happy to give her friend, the Chief of Police a call."

A cruiser pulled up in front of the inn twenty minutes later. There were two officers, one around her own age and the other a decade older. Marcie told her story to them. They then asked her questions, focusing particularly on how far the car had been from her when it swerved onto the shoulder of the road. Finally, after describing what had happened three times, Marcie asked them why they were so concerned with when the car had driven up on the shoulder of the road.

"It could have been a driver who fell asleep at the wheel," the older officer explained. "If he drove off the road a long time before reaching you, that would be a possibility."

"He didn't. He was going along just fine until he was a hundred feet from me, then he pulled onto the shoulder. He did it intentionally, this was no accident."

"Is there a reason why anyone would want to hurt you?" the younger officer asked.

Marcie explained what she was working on. The further into the explanation she got, the less plausible it began to sound. Would someone really attempt to kill her because she was looking into Jerry Kronberg's death? She could have been imagining it, but the two policemen seemed to have skeptical expressions as she came to the end of her story.

"So there's no one who's actually threatened you?" the older man asked.

Marcie shook her head.

"You didn't recognize the driver of the car?"

"Like I said, I think he was wearing a jacket with the hood up, so I couldn't see much of his face and head."

"And you have no idea of the make or model of the vehicle?"

"I wasn't paying attention, and when the car came right at me, I was too busy moving to look around. All I know is that it was a dark green sedan."

The man who walked into the lobby twenty minutes later wearing a business suit and flanked by two more policemen in uniform was rather short and thin, not fitting Marcie's idea of a police chief at all. But that's who he turned out to be. He came over, after talking for several minutes with the uniformed officers who'd questioned Marcie, and introduced himself to Marcie and Simon as Chief Broder.

He asked her once again to describe what had happened. Suppressing a sigh, Marcie repeated her story. A uniformed officer standing next to the Chief had a notebook out and seemed to be taking down her every word. The Chief asked for her to list all the people they'd talked to so far regarding the Kronberg case. Marcie couldn't tell by the expression on his face whether he thought any of them were likely suspects in the attack on her.

A uniformed officer walked across the lobby and whispered something in the Chief's ear.

"I sent a couple of officers out to the scene. The children-at-play sign you spotted enabled us to find the location pretty accurately. Fortunately it rained last night so the shoulder of the road was soft, and the car left deep tire tread marks. They confirm your story that the car left the road suddenly as it was approaching you."

Marcie barely refrained from saying, "of course my story is true."

"But it's still possible," the Chief continued, "that this was an accident. Somebody could have spilled coffee in his lap, been talking on his cell phone or dozed off just as he approached you. There are a number of reasons why someone might swerve off the road. However, it's also possible that this was intentional."

"Assuming it was intentional, is there any chance that you'll find out who it was?"

A somber look came over the Chief's face. "Without a better description of the driver or the car, I think it's very unlikely that we'll be able to apprehend the individual who did this."

Marcie nodded. "I was afraid that might be the case."

"It might be safest for you if you gathered together whatever information you have and left town."

Marcie felt a surge of anger sweep over her.

"Why should I have to leave town? I haven't done anything wrong."

"I know it doesn't seem fair, but there isn't much we can do. I'll tell the manager of the inn to have his staff be alert for anyone hanging around who doesn't belong. And I'll have a cruiser come by regularly to check on whether there's someone sitting nearby in a green car. Beyond that, there isn't much I can offer."

The Chief sat there with his hands open, palms up as if to prove how empty he was of ideas.

"Well, thank you, Chief," Marcie said, standing up and struggling to keep any sarcasm out of her voice. "I appreciate all the effort you're making."

The Chief nodded and walked over to the officers by the door and appeared to be giving them orders.

"Maybe we should leave town," Simon said as he and Marcie headed toward the elevator. "We have enough information to write a story even though we don't have all the answers."

"We don't have any of the answers," Marcie snapped. "Sure we can write a puff piece that gives the history of the black dog and then generally alludes to the fact that Kronberg saw the dog twice before he died. But we could have written that before we came down here. We need to find out more in order to justify this trip."

"Okay, you're the boss. But I don't think either one of us should go wandering around alone. Whenever we're not in our rooms, we should be together."

Marcie paused for a minute. "That sounds like a sensible idea," she admitted. Then she glanced at her watch. "We don't have enough time to get breakfast here. We've got an appointment with Harry Schmidt at nine-thirty. Let's stop at a fast food place along the way."

"I guess that's all right," Simon said, frowning.

"Don't worry; they'll probably have some kind of low calorie meal."

Forty-five minutes later and right on time, they pulled up in front of Harry Schmidt's address. It turned out to be a dentist's office with Schmidt's name displayed prominently on a shingle.

They went into the lobby and up to a glass window. The window rolled back to reveal a young woman dressed in a bright yellow smock. Marcie introduced herself and said they had an appointment with the doctor at nine-thirty. The woman consulted a daily calendar, then said she'd be right back. Two minutes later she returned to say that the doctor was running a little late and they should have a seat. There were no other patients in the waiting room, so they had their choice of seats around the large coffee table that filled the middle of the room. It was covered with magazines and other reading material. Simon picked up the local newspaper and began to read. Marcie sat there staring into space. Somewhere towards the back of the building, a drill started to whine.

"I hate dentists' offices. I hate the sounds, I hate the smell, I hate their looks. I pretty much hate everything about them."

"Have you had a lot of serious dental work done?" Simon asked.

She shook her head. "Only a couple of fillings, but that was enough. There's something about having someone's hands and a bunch of instruments in your mouth that creeps me out. Somehow it's all so...intimate. Much worse than when you go to your physician's; all he does is give you a couple of pokes and makes you take deep breaths. Not bad at all, compared to the dentist."

"But look on the bright side," Simon said, "dentistry today is pretty painless. When I was your age that wasn't true."

"Have you ever had a tooth taken out?"

"Once."

"You see, that's something else I don't like. The idea of permanently losing a part of your body."

"Today they can implant an artificial tooth that works just like the real one."

"It's not the same," Marcie said, a stubborn pout her face.

Simon went back to reading his paper, while Marcie stared, tight-lipped, across the room. Ten minutes later, the receptionist called them in. They walked down a hall past two rooms with large dental chairs in the center. At the end of the hall, the receptionist escorted them into an office with a desk and a couple of chairs for guests. The man behind the desk came around to greet them. He wasn't very tall, but he was powerfully built. Marcie shuddered at the thought of those strong hands wrestling a tooth from her mouth. When he shook hands, his grip was very gentle, which made her feel a little better. Before he sat down, Dr. Schmidt closed the door.

"I understand that you want to ask me some questions about Jerry."

"You were good friends?" Marcie asked.

"Yes. We'd been friends for about four years."

"How did you meet?"

"Actually we met when he came in with a toothache. This was shortly after he'd moved to Comford. Jerry didn't like dentists. Like a lot of people he was very afraid of dental pain, and he'd had some bad experiences in the past."

Marcie felt more than saw Simon glance at her. She kept her expression neutral.

"When I worked on him and he had no pain, he was very grateful. We began to talk and discovered that we were both devoted to the game of golf. I invited him to play at the country club, and eventually supported his application for membership."

"Were you were aware of the development of Three Star?"

"Oh yes, it was the talk of the country club. Everybody wanted in on it."

"Did you invest heavily in it?" asked Marcie.

The man shook his head and to Marcie's surprise appeared to blush.

"Actually I'm not invested at all."

"Why not?" Simon asked.

"It wasn't from the lack of trying. When almost everyone at the club was throwing money at Jerry, he never suggested to me that I invest. Finally I told him that I had some money set aside, and I'd like to put it in Three Star."

"What did he say?" asked Marcie.

"He said that it wasn't the right type of investment for me. There was too much risk involved. Then he recommended a couple of other places where I might put my money." Schmidt shook his head. "I have to admit that I was a little hurt that he wouldn't let me invest with him. Here were all these other people that he didn't know half as well, and they were getting terrific returns on their money. While I was supposed to invest in a fund that wasn't doing half as well."

"I take it that the fund you did invest in is still in business?" Simon asked.

Schmidt smiled. "Not an exciting investment, but one that's safe. In retrospect I can see that Jerry was trying to protect me."

"So he really was your friend," Marcie said.

"Yes. At first I couldn't believe what everyone was saying about him. But when the criminal charges were filed, it seemed pretty clear that he had bilked a lot of his friends and acquaintances."

"Did you talk with him frequently after the charges were filed?"

"We used to get together for lunch every two weeks or so at someplace outside of town where he wouldn't be recognized. We spent most of our time talking about our kids, our golf games, pretty much anything other than Jerry's legal problems. I think Jerry liked getting together with me because I was the only one of his friends who wouldn't mention the elephant in the dining room.'

"So you never talked about his legal situation?"

Schmidt folded his muscular hands in his lap, looking almost prayerful.

"The very last time we got together, which was the day before he died, we did. Jerry brought it up; he seemed to want to talk about it. He said that his lawyer was telling him that things didn't look good, and he'd probably end up serving significant prison time. He wasn't sure that he could handle that."

"Did he talk about committing suicide rather than going to jail?" asked Marcie.

"No, he didn't say anything like that. I'd say that he seemed a bit depressed but not suicidal."

"What else did he say about his situation?" Marci asked.

"He didn't give many details, but he indicated that he had some information that might be helpful to the authorities. He was hoping that he might be able to exchange it for less prison time."

"Did he say anything about the nature of this information?"

"Only that it would incriminate someone else. I think what he wanted to hash out with me was whether he should get another person in trouble in order to save himself."

"What did you tell him?"

"I told him that he had to consider his wife and the boys. If he could cut his sentence from fifteen years to five, he owed it to his family to talk to the authorities. After all, this other person's hands were hardly clean. He knew what he was getting into when he joined in the scheme."

"Did it seem like Jerry was going to take your advice?" asked Simon.

"It was hard to tell. He seemed very conflicted. If I had to guess, I'd say that he was probably going to talk to the authorities."

"And he gave you no idea about who this person could be?"

"Not a clue."

"Because you were so close to Jerry, did anyone ever think that you were part of the con?"

Schmidt paused for a moment. "When the charges came out, I think some people were cool towards me. I don't know if they thought I was part of the scheme or whether they were hostile to me because I was a friend of Jerry's."

"Any open accusations or threatening phone calls?"

Schmidt shook his head.

"Did Jerry talk with you about seeing the black dog on West Peak?" Marcie asked.

"After his first sighting of the dog, he laughed when he told me about it. We thought it was just some freakish coincidence. The second time he saw the dog was different. First of all it seemed like more than just a coincidence to have it happen again. Also that was the same day that Jeffrey Hunter took his own life. Jerry knew the story that the first time nothing happens; the second time something bad happens to someone close to you; the third time, you die."

"Did he seem afraid that the prophecy was going to come true?" asked Marcie.

"He seemed fatalistic about it. I suggested that if he just stopped hiking up West Peak that would be a sure way of avoiding the problem. But he said that he liked the hike, and if the prophecy was going to come true then it just would. He even laughed and said that seeing the black dog a third time might be better than spending the next decade or two in prison."

Marcie leaned forward in her chair. "Can you describe exactly what he saw when the dog appeared?"

"I don't remember all the details. I'm not even sure Jerry said that much about it. All I recall is that the dog would come out of the woods and run towards him where he was standing near the peak. When it was about halfway between him and the woods it would stop, turn around and run back into the trees."

"What kind of dog was it?"

"A small black dog. That's all Jerry said."

"Do you know anyone who has a black dog?"

"You think someone was trying to frighten Jerry? Why would anyone do that?"

"Maybe to get him to jump, or possibly to get him so off balance physically and emotionally that he'd be easy to push over the cliff."

"Well, I can't say that I know anyone who has a small black dog, but you usually don't know that kind of thing about people unless you visit them at their homes. Not many people in this part of Connecticut travel around with their dogs. I think that's more of a country western thing."

"Is there anything else you can tell us about Jerry that would help us to discover what happened to him?"

"I'll tell you what I've said to other people who've asked me how I could stay Jerry's friend. He was basically a good man, but not the strongest of men. When he moved to Comford, he was at loose ends. He'd worked in Manhattan for an investment company for ten years, and they let him go in a big downsizing. He came here with just enough money to get a mortgage on a house and a country club membership. This scheme was his last chance to be a success: to meet his mortgage payments and send his sons to a good college. He didn't want to cheat people. After a while, I think he believed he was really helping people by getting them to invest in Three Star. That was what made him such a good salesman. He believed his own con."

"But he didn't believe it enough to let you invest," Marcie said.

"That's true," Schmidt admitted. He smiled sadly. "I guess I make excuses for him because I really cared for the guy."

"There are worse reasons," said Marcie.

Schmidt started to say more, then just nodded his head.

Chapter 14

Stanley Wilkie sat in his kitchen and stared at the man across the counter from him. Having someone else in the house seemed very odd. It had been weeks, maybe months since anyone other than himself had been in the house.

Even before Three Star had gone down in flames, he rarely had company. He'd been divorced for two years and his wife, Marsha, had custody of their three children. Even when he'd visited the kids, he usually took them to places other than the house, and returned them to Marsha at nightfall. Now, with criminal charges about to be made against him, he didn't feel like seeing the children at all. The last time he'd tried to explain to them what had happened while putting himself in the most positive possible light, it hadn't gone well. Now a weekly phone call was the inadequate substitute. Since neither Marsha nor the children commented on his failure to visit, he thought that they were all just as happy not to spend time with a soon-to-be-indicted felon. Two of the children were in their teens, and he imagined that they were suffering at the hands of their peer group and probably blaming him for ruining their lives.

He looked around the kitchen and remembered the day four years ago when he and Marsha had picked out what was to be the kitchen of their dreams. He tried to retrieve the happiness and sense of promise they'd shared that day. He could remember those feelings, label them in his mind, but not experience them. The building of the house had given them a common purpose. Now, looking back, he realized that the project had been their last effort to stay together. Once the house was completed, they were forced to recognize that they no longer really cared for each other, leaving the house as a kind of museum to a way of life that no longer existed.

It was a shame that the kitchen with its granite counters, stainless steel, professional grade appliances, and trendy lighting was never used, Stanley thought. He certainly didn't use it. He either had take-out or went early in the morning to the mostly empty supermarket to buy frozen dinners that he would microwave. The sameness of the food simply reinforced the sameness of his days. Although he would experience moments of terror at the thought of going to prison, at other times he wondered how much worse it could be than the prison he currently occupied. Slowly his days had lost all structure. Sometimes he didn't get dressed until the afternoon, sometimes not at all. Before, his days had been scheduled around a few hours in the morning spent at the computer tracking his personal investments and calling his broker, followed by lunch and an occasional round of golf at the club. Serving on the boards of a couple of charities filled in the rest of his time and, he thought, earned him the respect of his community. He had been content.

Why had he ever gotten involved in Three Star? The best answer he could come up with was that Jerry had approached him shortly after Marsha had filed for divorce. In the time leading up to her decision to ask for a divorce, there had been almost constant sniping between them. One theme that Marsha harped upon was that he'd never really done anything with his life. He'd inherited several million, she would say, and all he had done was keep from losing it in bad investments. His father, she liked to say, had been the person responsible for the family wealth; Stanley's only accomplishment had been to live long enough to inherit it.

There had been enough truth to that remark that it got under his skin. He began to fantasize about making a killing in the market that would show Marsha just how smart and savvy he could be. So when Jerry approached him with the Three Star scheme, he was already half sold on any plan that would multiply his millions. Would he have done the same thing under different circumstances, if, for example, he and Marsha and the kids had still been together as a family? He didn't think so. Not because of the unethical nature of the plan because he knew himself well enough to realize that wouldn't have stopped him. But the fear of getting caught and the lack of a driving need for money would have made him too passive to get involved. He wondered, not for the first time, whether Jerry had sensed something in him that made him ripe for the plucking as a potential partner. In a way, he and Jeff Hunter had been deceived as much as those who invested in Three Star because they'd been told that there was a clear exit strategy that would enable them to wrap up the scheme, leaving no one the wiser. Yes, he'd been conned by Jerry and by the man sitting across from him.

"Drink your coffee," the man said, giving him an encouraging smile.

Stanley wondered why he'd come. He arrived at mid-morning, ringing the bell until Stan had rolled out of bed to see what was wrong. Then he'd said that Stan should get dressed while he made coffee. When Stanley came down fifteen minutes later, he was greeted by the smell of fresh brewed coffee and the slightly burnt aroma of toast. They made him suddenly realize how hungry he was. He was now on his second cup of coffee and third piece of toast.

"You shouldn't be living like this," the man said. "It's not healthy being this isolated. Everything seems worse when you don't have anyone to talk to."

"That's easy for you to say." Stanley meant his words to be sharp, but somewhere between his brain and his mouth they seemed to soften and become slurry. "You aren't under indictment."

"That's true,"

"It's my life that's going to be ruined, not yours."

The man nodded. "You know sometimes when a man is drowning, he'll grab onto anyone near him out of a desperate hope to be saved, and all that accomplishes is that both of them drown."

Stanley tried to focus on what the man had said, but his mind was sluggish and the sentence seemed just too long for him to comprehend.

"What's your point?" he asked in bewilderment.

The man smiled. "Are you feeling sleepy?"

Stanley realized that he suddenly did feel very sleepy. He'd never known coffee to make him feel sleepy before. He wanted to put his head down on the expensive granite counter and close his eyes.

"To get back to your question, my point is that mentioning my name to the authorities would not improve your position, and it would greatly damage mine. So we'd both end up drowning."

"Drowning," Stanley repeated.

"Yes. Do you know what someone has to do when a drowning person clings to them?"

Stanley shook his head.

"He has to fight to free himself, even if that means that the other man drowns. Do you understand me?"

"Need to get some sleep," Stanley said, getting to his feet and leaning on the counter so he wouldn't fall to the floor.

The man walked around the counter and put his arm around Stanley's waist.

"You know, this is a very lovely home. Why don't you show me around?"

"Need to sleep."

"You'll get all the sleep you need after the tour." Lifting Stanley up and half-dragging his feet across the floor, the man said, "Why don't we begin the tour in an organized way by starting in the basement and working our way up to your bedroom? Is that okay?"

Stanley's head nodded loosely.

"Good. I thought it might be. Shall we go?" the man said.

Chapter 15

Sheila Little opened the front door. She smiled in a sort of general way at the two of them, then focused what seemed to be a special smile on Simon. Even though Marcie rarely paid much attention to fashion, she noticed that Sheila was wearing a pair of form-fitting jeans with a snug blue sweater, both of which helped to accentuate her generous curves. Her shoes had a sizeable heel, bringing her close to Simon's six feet. Standing there next to her, Marcie felt like a dwarf.

"I thought that we'd have lunch first, then discuss the case. Chef Susan will be serving us," Sheila whispered, hinting at the need to be discrete as she led them down the hall.

The chef seemed to know by telepathy when they were all seated around the table, and she brought in their salads. This was followed by scrod in a delicious crème sauce. True to her plan, Sheila moved the conversation in a safe direction. She talked about her role as a friend of the local library, and her responsibilities as a board member of her late husband's company. The more she talked, the more Marcie thought that Sheila had a quick mind and the self-confidence necessary to make her a skilled decision-maker. Unlike her husband, she seemed unimpressed by people who were better educated or more experienced than herself, and Marcie could easily picture her standing up to any board of directors.

Sheila even got Simon to talk about *Tristram Shandy* after reassuring him several times that she really was interested in the theme of his book. Simon started out hesitantly, but as he got into it, his voice took on a fervor that Marcie hadn't heard before, and he seemed positively energized. She could picture him being a very effective teacher. For her part, Sheila was giving him the rapt attention of a skilled listener. Marcie suspected that, if Sheila liked books as much as she claimed, she'd found a fruitful avenue for deepening her relationship with Simon.

When they finished the homemade raspberry sherbet that concluded the meal, Sheila led them back down the hall to the study where they had talked last time. She carefully closed the door behind them and immediately turned to Marcie.

"How are you? Did you get injured by that car?"

Marcie shook her head. "I'm fine. Just a few scratches."

"And you have no idea who it was?"

"It all happened very fast, and the driver was wearing a hoodie, so I didn't get a good look at his face."

Sheila sat down in one of the leather chairs and tapped her fingers on the arm.

"Are you sure you want to continue this investigation? It seems to have taken an ugly turn."

"I'm not ready to throw in the towel yet," Marcie said. "Simon and I will stay close together, and I won't be engaging in any more morning runs."

"She won't be doing any more of them because she isn't likely to get me to come along," said Simon.

"There's a nice workout room in the inn that we can use," Marcie said, and smiled to herself as Simon frowned.

"Well, I'm glad that you're all right," Sheila said. "What did you learn from Florence Lee?"

Marcie summarized the conversation. "Overall, I got the impression that Florence isn't sure whether the three men under indictment are the only ones involved. But so far she hasn't been able to come up with the name of a fourth partner. I think she's still actively looking. She also isn't sure whether Kronberg was murdered or committed suicide."

"What did you find out from Floyd Schmidt?" asked Sheila.

"Well, he definitely has a more positive view of Jerry Kronberg than anyone else. That might be due to the fact that Kronberg never let him invest in Three Star," Marcie replied.

"I'd heard that rumor, but didn't know if was true. Do you think he was involved in the con? Could he be the fourth partner?"

Marcie shrugged. "I don't know for sure, of course, but he seems like a real straight arrow. And I'd imagine that the prosecutor's office has already taken a hard look at him."

"That would be my impression of Floyd as well. He's my dentist, and I'd certainly never suspect him of wrong doing."

"What about Steve Pawling? Do you think he would hate Kronberg enough to kill him?" asked Simon.

"How did you come to meet Steve?" asked Sheila.

Simon explained about the conversation in the inn dining room.

"It's a sad story. When Steven's mother died, the heirs were Steven and his brother and two sisters. Steven was appointed the executor of the estate. I think his mother had selected him because he was the only child who continued to live in the area. Steven hired Charles Foster to get the will through probate. Once the estate had been divided up, Steven convinced his siblings to let him invest much of what they had received in Three Star. Now they're suing

Steven, claiming that he misled them about the risks involved. Charles is representing Steven."

"I'm surprised he would hire Jerry Kronberg's brother-in-law," said Marcie.

"Charles represented the Pawling family long before Jerry moved to Comford," Shelia said. "He's been in practice here for twenty years, and handles the legal work for several people whom Jerry bilked."

"So, has the pressure of the lawsuit driven Steven to imbibe too much?" Simon asked.

"I think he's had a tendency to drink too much ever since he was in college. But let's say that his current circumstances have made the condition worse. He was never very close to his sisters and brother; they were quite a bit older than he, but he does feel guilty over what happened. Steven has drifted from one mediocre sales job to another since leaving school, and I think he felt that investing the family inheritance wisely was his last chance to prove himself."

"He must have been furious with Kronberg," said Marcie.

Sheila smiled slightly. "He always refers to him as 'the sleaze.'"

"So I noticed," Marcie said. "Do you think when he's sober that he might be capable of acting on his anger?"

"You're back to asking if I think Jerry was murdered. As I told you before, I think it was suicide. And as to whether Steven could have killed Jerry, I'm not sure that Steven could get himself organized enough to carry out that kind of plan. Even when he's sober, he's somewhat diffuse. It's just a really sad situation. Poor Steven was trying to do his best for the family by investing with Jerry."

"And when it all went bad, his siblings decided to sue him?" asked Marcie.

"Yes. Now they say that they never gave him permission to invest so much or that he didn't perform due diligence before investing. Like Steven would know from due diligence; right now he's a car salesman. He was just following along behind all the big shots who thought they knew about investing and got fooled anyway. His family should just admit that they were greedy and made a bad investment. It's time to let it go. Charlie Foster is a good lawyer; I've used him a few times myself. I hope he's able to get him off."

"You really don't think Pawling could have killed Jerry?" asked Marcie.

"Even when he's sober, which is becoming more and more infrequent, from what I hear, I don't think he has the spine to kill anyone."

"He could just be a good actor, pretending to be the ineffectual drunk," said Simon.

Sheila nodded. "That's possible. But I've known him since he was a boy, and his behavior is right in character. I don't think he's acting."

"I guess we can take him off our list," Marcie said.

"But there is one thing..." Sheila began.

"What?"

"Steven does have a black dog. A small dog that he dotes on, a mix of Chihuahua and something else. I know because he used to sneak the dog into the country club where they have a strict no pets policy."

"Why would he do that?" Simon asked.

"Because he could. They were never going to throw him out; his father was one of the club's charter members. The worst that ever happened was that he was asked to take the dog outside."

"That sounds like adolescent rebelliousness," said Simon.

Sheila shook her head. "He still does it, and he's in his late twenties."

"Arrested development, then," Simon said. "Do you think having a black dog makes him a suspect?"

"I don't think it means much. If Jerry actually did see a black dog up there, it was surely some stray and not Steven's pampered pet," said Sheila. "Plus I can't imagine Steven making the climb up to West Peak even when sober. If we were talking about someone spray painting Kronberg's house or breaking his windows, I'd say Steve could be our man. But murder seems to be out of his league."

Marcie nodded and frowned in frustration.

"Do you have anyone left to get in touch with?" Sheila asked.

"There's still Stanley Wilkie. He doesn't seem to answer his phone," Marcie said. As if to prove it, she took out her cell phone and punched in the number. "Goes directly to voicemail."

"He's probably gotten his share of harassing phone calls, so it's not surprising that he wouldn't answer. I've heard that he doesn't leave the house very often either. He's another sad case. His wife asked for a divorce shortly before he invested with Kronberg. I think he went in with Jerry because he wanted to appear successful and show his wife what she was missing out on."

"Instead she probably thanks her lucky stars that she got the divorce when she did," said Simon.

"The scandal is bad enough as it is for her and the children," Sheila said. "Yolanda Kronberg and her two boys are no doubt suffering as well."

"What about Jeffrey Hunter?" asked Simon. "Did he have any family?"

Sheila shook her head, "Not in the area. I've heard that he had a wife and kids back in

Boston, but got divorced shortly before moving out here."

"I would really like to have a chance to talk to Stanley Wilkie," Marcie said. "He has an insider's knowledge of what's been going on. He might be able to give me the name of someone who's threatened both Jerry and himself."

"I'd recommend that you go right to his house and knock on the door," Sheila said. "If you're persistent enough, he might talk to you. He's not the brightest light going. His money was inherited from his father who had a company that made furniture. The father's gift for business wasn't passed on to Stanley. He sold the company and has been basically living on his investments ever since."

"I like your idea of going to his house," said Marcie. "It will make me harder to ignore."

"And once he finds out that you aren't there to write a piece trashing him, he might be more forthcoming. He doesn't live far from here."

Sheila went over to the desk and began writing out the directions.

"I'd still like to know who among the people defrauded owns a black dog," said Marcie. "I still don't think Jerry's seeing that dog on West Peak was just a coincidence."

"I could talk to the Chief. Maybe he could have someone call all the people who were defrauded and ask if anyone has a black dog,"

Sheila said, walking over to hand Marcie the directions.

"I'd appreciate that," Marcie said. She turned to Simon. "Maybe we could check at the animal pound to see if any stray black dogs have been picked up or if anyone has left a black dog at the pound in the last couple of weeks."

"Just go a quarter of a mile past your inn going west and you'll find the pound," Sheila said.

Marcia stood up. "Thank you again for lunch, Sheila. Now I think it's time for us to ratchet up the pressure on Wilkie."

"It was my pleasure," said Sheila, taking a long look at Simon, who gave her a big smile.

"Would the two of you be free to come to dinner tonight?"

Marcie glanced at Simon who gave her a noncommittal look. "We don't want to impose," she said.

"Oh, you wouldn't be. I can have Susan make enough for three, then I'll just heat it up for us. I may not be a genius in the kitchen, but I'm pretty good at using the microwave."

"Well, that will be fine, then," Marcie said. "Thank you. I'm sure we'll both be looking forward to it."

Sheila looked at Simon who nodded, and Marcie thought that she detected a faint blush.

*****

Amanda glanced away from the window and down at the computer screen. She realized with a start that she had no recollection of what she had been working on. She read the paragraph in front of her and remembered that it was an article about the mills in Lowell. It was actually quite a good piece, but Amanda knew it would take more than a good story to get her mind off her problems.

She'd been rerunning last night's meeting with Richard over and over in her mind. She had gotten what she wanted, a stay of execution, she thought with a grim smile. But Richard wasn't going to be satisfied until they had set a firm date, and he was clearly focused on October, which was only seven months away. Seven months that to Amanda seemed to be the blink of an eye. *In the fall I'll be getting married,* she said to herself. The words had a finality to them that made her shudder. And Richard wanted to see her again tonight. She'd almost told him that they should cool it and only see each other a couple of times a week. But the ring on her finger told her that she couldn't say that. An engaged couple wanted to be together. When they were apart they spent much of their time looking forward to being together. What kind of fiancée was she that she didn't want to spend more time with the man who was to be her husband? What kind of wife would she be if she couldn't stand seeing her husband every day? *What kind of person am I that I lie to a person who loves me?* she asked herself.

Amanda pressed down hard on the top of her desk, trying to keep in touch with reality. She suddenly felt very calm, now that she had reached the heart of the problem that had been bothering her for the last two days. She had lied to Richard when she said that she wanted to marry him. She liked him a lot, maybe even loved him, but right now she had no desire to get married. It wouldn't be right to get Richard to agree to a longer engagement when she wasn't even sure that she wanted to be married. If she told him the truth and he got angry and said he never wanted to see her again, she'd have to deal with it. A painful truth was better than this lie. Having made up her mind, Amanda found that she could return to the article.

Chapter 16

Marcie mashed her thumb into the doorbell one more time. She heard chimes somewhere in the back of the house ring out a complicated little tune. Simon shifted nervously from foot to foot.

"I'm not comfortable doing this," he said. "To keep ringing the bell amounts to harassment."

"You can't always be polite when you're trying to put together a story. If Wilkie feels harassed, let him call the police," Marcie said, ringing the bell again.

There was still no answer and the ornate double door stayed closed.

"Let's go around back."

"Wouldn't that be trespassing?"

Marcie shrugged. "We can always say that we were just checking to see if he was in the back yard and didn't hear us."

Marcie followed the walkway and marched around to the rear of the house. There she rang the bell again and peeked in through the windows in the door.

"See anything?" Simon asked.

"Just part of a large fancy kitchen."

Marcie reached down and tried the door handle. She was surprised when the door swung open.

"We shouldn't..." Simon began, but by then Marcie had already moved inside the house and was shouting, "Mr. Wilkie! Mr. Wilkie! We're from *Roaming New England* magazine."

Soon they found themselves standing in the middle of the kitchen.

"It's odd that he would leave the back door open," said Marcie.

"He probably didn't expect to have an aggressive visitor like you."

"Well, he should. After all, he's going to be indicted on several felonies involving his friends and neighbors. I'd sure lock my door under those circumstances."

"Anyway, let's get out of here before he comes home."

"I want to make sure he isn't here."

"Are you serious?"

Marcie gave him a long look. "If you want to wait outside or back in the car, go ahead, but I want to make sure that he's not hiding somewhere."

Before Simon could reply, Marcie went down the front hall, calling out the man's name.

Reluctantly he tagged along behind. They reached the large two-story foyer where there was a grand staircase leading up to the second floor.

"He doesn't seem to be down here," Marcie said. "I suppose he could be asleep upstairs. Why don't I check up there while you look in the basement?"

Simon's face took on a stubborn expression.

"Or suit yourself," Marcie said, ascending the stairway.

Marcie found that the second floor consisted of four bedrooms, three bathrooms and a bonus room that featured a pool table. The largest bedroom, which Marcie assumed must be the master, contained an unmade king-sized bed. Probably that's where Wilkie sleeps, Marcie thought. It looks like he was here last night, but he doesn't appear to be home right now. Marcie went down the stairs, and as she headed along the hall to the kitchen, she saw Simon coming towards her. He started to say something but the words didn't quite come out. He coughed, like a man about to give a speech, then tried again.

"I think I've found Wilkie. He's downstairs."

Marcie brushed past him headed for the cellar stairs, but Simon grabbed her arm roughly.

"You don't want to go down there."

"Why not?"

"Because he's dead."

The two officers in uniform who responded to Marcie's call were the same younger/older team that had talked to Marcie when she'd almost been run down. They gave her a fishy look when she explained why they were in the house.

"So you just walked in because the door was open?" the older cop asked.

"We thought that Mr. Wilkie might have been in trouble."

"Did you have any reason to believe that? Did you hear him call out?"

"No," Marcie replied.

"Are you sticking to the same story?" he asked Simon.

"That's what happened."

The cop glared at him. "I would have thought that at least *you* would have had better sense."

Simon looked down, but didn't say anything.

"And when would you have found the body if we hadn't come inside?" Marcie shot back.

The cop didn't say anything. He just turned away.

Marcie and Simon sat at the kitchen counter waiting as the police made calls and stood in the lobby, as if expecting that at any moment they'd be called upon to keep out a crowd.

"You didn't touch anything down there, did you?"

Simon shook his head. "I saw him hanging from the pipe, and got out of there right away."

"Did you see anything else?"

"There was a small kitchen ladder lying on its side right below where he was hanging. It sure looks like suicide."

"Now all the stars of Three Star are dead. Two appear to be suicides, and Jerry's is whatever it is."

"I guess it could be three suicides," Simon said softly.

"But wouldn't you think at least one of them would have wanted his day in court?"

Simon shrugged. "Just as everyone has been saying, these guys aren't hardened criminals. The prospect of serious prison time could have pushed them over the edge."

Marcie stood up and began to walk around the kitchen. She was disturbed by the fact that she hadn't ignored Simon and gone downstairs to see the body for herself. Had that been a sign of weakness in her, an inability to face her fears? She was sure her father would say so. But she'd seen enough things on this job that kept her awake at night, she didn't want to voluntarily add another. She looked over at Simon, who seemed to be examining the pattern in the tile floor, and wondered if he would spend a lifetime regretting that he had followed her into the house.

She let her eyes sweep over the counter, admiring the dark green veins in the granite, then she looked at the various appliances located along its periphery. Marcie stopped to stare at the clear glass coffee carafe. She took a dish towel, and, glancing over her shoulder to see that no police were watching her, she picked up the carafe and held it up to the light coming in the window.

"I don't think you should do that," Simon whispered urgently.

Marcie put the carafe back in place, then walked over to Simon.

"I think someone has made coffee today. There's moisture in the bottom of the pot, like someone rinsed it out and left it to dry."

"Maybe Wilkie used it this morning."

"You mean he made himself a pot of coffee, then decided to commit suicide?"

"It's possible."

"Then he washed his cup, put it away, and rinsed out the coffee pot?"

"I remember hearing somewhere that people often straighten up their rooms before they kill themselves. They want to leave everything neat."

"Or maybe Wilkie had coffee with someone earlier today, and that person killed him."

Simon gave a little twitch. "That's just speculation."

Marcie was about to reply when the front door opened and Chief Broder moved swiftly down the front hall. He gave Marcie a long look, then turned and went down the stairs to the basement. When he returned a few minutes later, he came into the kitchen and took a seat at the round table in front of the slider to the back yard. He gestured for Marcie to join him, and asked Simon to take a seat outside on the deck.

When Marcie was seated at the table, the Chief gave her a stern look. "How about you take it from pulling up in front of the house, and run through what happened?"

After Marcie had completed her description of events, the Chief sat there for a moment tapping his finger on the tabletop.

"You know, if you weren't a friend of Sheila's, you might be in big trouble now."

Marcie remained silent, deciding that this wasn't the time to present a defense of her actions.

"It also doesn't hurt your case that Wilkie's death is so clearly a suicide."

"Do you really think so?" Marcie couldn't resist asking.

The Chief raised an eyebrow. "You don't think it is?"

Marcie explained her coffeepot theory.

"People do all sorts of different things before taking their lives. I don't think your evidence is conclusive."

"How about just being suggestive?"

The Chief shrugged.

Marcie frowned and folded her arms across her chest. An idea that had been just outside her consciousness suddenly popped into place.

"You found traces of sedatives in Jeffrey Hunter's system, am I right?"

"Yes. There were traces of a commonly used sedative. He had taken a sizeable overdose."

"Did you find a prescription bottle?"

He shook is head. "No, but we found a small plastic bag with some left in it on his nightstand."

"Had his doctor prescribed them?"

"No. But today it's easy enough to get all kinds of drugs over the Internet. It wouldn't surprise me that he might have had trouble sleeping and purchased some that way."

"So you figure he took the pills, then when he got sleepy, he sat in the car with the engine running?"

"That's our hypothesis."

"Couldn't someone else have drugged him without his knowledge, then carried the body out to the car and started the engine?"

"Of course, but there was no evidence indicating that anyone else was with him at the time."

"And what if you discover that Wilkie also had a sedative in his system at the time of death?"

The Chief paused. "It would probably bother me a little because I don't like coincidences.

But studies show that lots of suicides take drugs or use liquor in order to build up the courage. And anyway, who would want these men dead?"

"How about the people they've swindled?"

"They're angry all right, but I don't think they've gone as far as wanting to commit murder. We did check on the whereabouts of several of the more vocal ones at the time of Hunter's murder and even at the time of Kronberg's death. Some of them had good alibis, some didn't. But you can't expect every person to be in the presence of others during the time frame of a murder."

"What about the possibility that there was a fourth partner in Three Star? He would want to keep his identity a secret, and be afraid that one of the three would sell him out to the prosecution in exchange for a lighter sentence."

"From what I've heard from federal prosecutors there is some evidence, mostly e-mails, that might be interpreted in such a way as to indicate a fourth partner. I know Florence Lee has that bee in her bonnet. I've heard that she was leaning on Wilkie to see if he'd talk, and she's been working hard to get the prosecutors to dig into the matter."

"With all the partners dead, there isn't anywhere to dig now."

"I guess there are lots of e-mails that haven't been examined yet. The prosecutor thinks he's looked at enough to win his case, but Florence wants all of them examined because she thinks that somewhere, someone said something that will reveal who the fourth partner was."

"So maybe three dead partners isn't enough," Marcie said.

The Chief stared at her. "Tell your friend to come on inside. It's your turn to enjoy the lovely weather."

"One more thing, Chief. I know that Sheila requested that you check with the people defrauded by Three Star to find out who has a black dog. How's that search coming?"

"We called the department of licensing and checked the names of the people defrauded against a list of those with licensed dogs. There turned out to be twelve people who were defrauded by Kronberg who also own dogs. I have a man visiting each residence to actually eyeball the animal. I'll let Sheila know if any of them are black."

Marcie went out on the deck and sent Simon inside. As she sat there she thought to herself once again that finding the black dog might be the only way to solve the murders.

Chapter 17

"Are you okay?" Marcie asked. Since leaving Wilkie's house, Simon had said nothing. She couldn't tell if he was angry with her about something or still struggling with what he'd seen in the basement.

"How can you ask that?" he said in a dead voice.

"Are you upset with me?"

"Of course, I am. You dragged me into that house where I had one of the worst experiences of my life."

"I was just doing my job," said Marcie.

Simon gave a short laugh. "I thought our job was to do some research on a legendary tale, throwing in a bit of recent history to give it some punch. I didn't realize we had to take the place of the police."

"I see what I'm doing as a form of investigative journalism. I'm trying to find out if what happened really supports the legend or could plausibly have come about in another way."

Simon rubbed a hand over his face and sighed.

"Where are we going next?"

"To the pound. I want to see if anyone has adopted a black dog in the last six months."

"Why only six months?"

"I figure that's about the maximum length of time you'd need in order to train a mature dog to obey. If somebody did get a dog with the intention of using him on West Peak, he wouldn't want to have the dog around any longer than necessary. People might see the dog and associate it with him or her."

"What do we do once we've got a list of the people who've adopted black dogs?"

"We pay them a visit to see."

Simon lapsed back into silence. After driving for another ten minutes they pulled up in front of a long low building. At one end there was a yard surrounded by a chain link fence. In back of the building was a large grass field. Through the open windows that ran along the top of the building they could hear barking.

"I'm staying out of this. I'll let you do all the talking," Simon said, as they got out of the car and walked up to the front door

When they walked inside there was a small waiting room with hard plastic chairs. On one wall was a glass window that was rolled back to reveal an office with a desk in the middle. A young woman wearing jeans and a flannel shirt popped up from behind a desk at the sound of the door. As they looked more closely, a small brown dog peeked from around the side.

"Just giving Oscar a little scratch behind the ears," she explained.

Marcie smiled. "Maybe you can help me."

"Are you interested in adopting a dog or cat?'

"Not exactly. I'm actually looking for a dog that may have been adopted."

The woman gave her a puzzled glance.

Marcie grinned. "It's a long story, but basically my Aunt Sally's dog ran away about six months ago. My aunt lives by herself and she's not quite as with it as she used to be, so aside from wandering around the neighborhood calling out the dog's name, she just sat at home feeling miserable. We only found out yesterday when we came to visit that the dog has disappeared. My aunt never thought to come to the pound, and since Sally doesn't drive, that would have been hard for her to do anyway. So we've decided to give her a hand."

Marcie stared meaningfully at Simon who reluctantly nodded his head.

"What does your aunt's dog look like?"

"Black and on the small to medium side," said Marcie.

"We have only one black dog here right now, and he's pretty big. But you can take a look at him if you want."

"How long has he been here?"

"Only two weeks, but you don't know how long your aunt's dog was roaming free before he got picked up by animal control. It could still be him."

"Why don't we take a look anyway?"

Tammy opened the door for them and they went down a short hall, where she opened a large metal door. Immediately Marcie's senses were assaulted by sounds and smells. Both sides of the long narrow room were lined with cages, and in most cases there was a dog standing at the front of the cage looking out at the visitors as if knowing here was a potential family to join. Marcie tried not to get distracted by all the sweet faces staring at her, and she followed closely behind Tammy who walked halfway down on the right side. In the cage was a black dog that was clearly a mixture of German shepherd and something else. He stared at Marcie with solemn brown eyes.

Never having seen the dog on West Peak, she was guessing, but Marcie didn't think this dog would meet anyone's criteria for smallness.

"He's a beautiful animal," she said regretfully, "but he isn't my aunt's."

She stared at Simon. "Definitely not," he finally added.

"It was a long shot," said Tammy. "Let's go into the office where we keep a computer file with a picture of each dog that gets adopted.

You can go through all the pictures for the last six months and see what you find."

"Sounds great."

"What's the point of doing this?" Simon whispered as Tammy walked on ahead. "The police are already checking on dog owners who were defrauded by Kronberg."

"Just a hunch," Marcie whispered. Tammy stopped to look back at them, and Marcie gave her a smile. "Let's talk later," she said.

They went into the small office. Tammy sat in front of her computer and opened a file. She scrolled through it until she came to a date six months prior. Then she showed them how to click on the name of each dog and bring up its picture and the identity of the person who'd adopted it, and how to send the information to the printer. After watching them for a few minutes to make sure they had a handle on things, she said that she had to take some of the dogs out for a walk, and she'd be back in twenty minutes.

There had been forty-seven dogs adopted in the last six months. After rejecting some of them for color or size, they were left with five small black dogs. They printed out the information for each.

"Now would you explain to me why we're doing all this?" asked Simon.

"I figured that if someone did get a black dog purposely to spook Kronberg, he wouldn't want the dog to be traceable back to him. Getting him at a pet shop or from a breeder would involve paying with a credit card, check or in cash. Paying in cash would be the only method that would conceal his identity, but it might make him easy to remember because few people pay with cash for such a large purchase."

"You mean he was afraid that the police might check to see where a black dog was purchased?"

"Right. And I bet Chief Broder will do that as soon as he's checked out the fraud victims' dogs."

"So what did our guy do to hide his identity?"

"I'm betting that he got someone else to make the purchase for him."

"From here?"

"Or possibly a pet store. A breeder would probably be too fussy to let someone adopt without references of some kind."

"So now we check out these five dogs. But how do we know which one was used at West Peak? After all, we never saw the dog, and we don't know its name."

"If I'm right, we won't have to, because the person who bought the dog won't have it any more. They'll have given it to the guy who frightened Kronberg."

They stopped talking as Tammy closed the large door behind her and stepped into the office.

"Find any good leads?" she asked.

Marcie showed her the five printouts.

"I remember a couple of these," Tammy said. She pointed to one of them. "This dog went to a family where the boy wanted a dog. He was a cute kid, and it was love at first sight. You know, technically the dog belongs to the people who adopted it. We keep the dog for a month in case the original owner shows up. After that the dog belongs to us, and we sell it to the adoptive family for a nominal fee."

"So what you're saying is that even if we find my aunt's dog, we can't take it back without the current owner's permission," said Marcie.

Tammy nodded. "I know it sounds harsh, but we've got to have rules."

"Don't worry, if we find the right dog we'll offer a good amount of money to get it back."

"And what if they refuse?" Simon asked.

"Then we'll just have to get Aunt Sally a new dog," Marcie replied, giving him a look that told him to drop it. "Now how are we going to find our way to each of these places?"

Tammy showed her how to go online and generate a map for each of the locations. When they were done, they thanked the young woman and headed back to their car.

"We're not really going to try to take someone's dog away, are we?" asked Simon.

"Of course not. We're interested in the person who bought the dog for someone else."

The first house that they stopped at was less than half a mile from the pound. It was a ranch with a bicycle in the driveway and a van in the open garage.

"Are we sticking with the Aunt Sally story?" asked Simon unhappily.

Marcie nodded.

They rang the doorbell and in a minute or two a woman in her thirties opened the door.

"Can I help you?" she asked.

Marcie told her the story about Aunt Sally and her missing dog. As the woman listened, her expression became more troubled. When Marcie was done, she said, "I'm sorry for your aunt, but you realize that the dog is ours now. It would break my son's heart to give him up."

"Let's not worry about that just yet," Marcie said soothingly. "It may not even be the same dog."

The woman turned and called to the back of the house, "Jason would you bring Potter here for a minute?"

"Potter?" said Simon.

The woman smiled slightly. "He's crazy about those books."

A boy who looked to be around ten came down the hall carrying a small black dog in his arms. He stood beside his mother and stared at the strangers warily as if he sensed that they meant trouble.

"He could be the one," said Marcie. "I don't really remember exactly what the dog looked like, but I know his name, "Hi there, Marty. Who's a good dog?"

The dog looked at her blankly.

"Hi, Marty. Come here, Marty," she tried again.

The dog turned his face up to the boy's as if asking who 'Marty' was supposed to be.

"I don't think it's your aunt's dog," said the woman, relief evident in her voice.

"Apparently not," Marcie said. "Thank you for your time."

"Well, that was painful," Simon said after the door closed behind them.

"C'mon, it's not like we're actually going to take anyone's dog away. Maybe we'll get lucky at our next stop."

No one was home at the next house, but when they rang the bell, they could hear a dog begin to bark, so they crossed it off their list. At the next house a tall thin woman came to the door and looked at them as if unhappy that she had opened the door at all. Marcie launched into her story, and as it went along, the woman appeared more and more uncomfortable. When Marcie concluded with a request to see the dog, the woman appeared undecided as to whether she wanted to talk any further or slam the door in their faces.

"The dog really meant the world to my aunt," Marcie said, leaning forward so her body was in the doorway.

"I can't help you," the woman said.

"Can we at least see your dog?" asked Marcie.

"No," the woman paused as if trying to decide whether to say anything further. "I don't have him anymore."

"Where did he go? What happened?" Marcie asked.

"It's a long story."

"I'd really like to hear it if it will help us locate Marty."

The woman sighed. "I was coming out of the unemployment office when this man came up to me and asked if I'd like to make some money. He wanted to get a dog for his niece. He planned to adopt a dog from the pound, but his ex-wife's sister worked there, and he thought she would give him a hard time. He asked me if I'd get the dog for him. He offered me five hundred dollars. All I had to do was follow him to the pound, get a dog, which had to be small and black, then hand it over to him out in the parking lot. That's what I did, and he paid me."

"Do you have any way of getting in touch with him?" Marcie asked.

She shook her head.

"What did he look like?"

"Middle-aged, brown hair, pretty tall, there was nothing very remarkable about him, and it's been six months since I've seen him."

"So you have no idea where the dog is now?" asked Marcie.

"I'm sorry. I'd like to help you."

"And your name is?" asked Marcie.

"Barbara Lieber."

Marcie took out her pad and scribbled her own name and phone number. She handed the sheet to the woman, asking her to get in touch if she remembered anything else.

"Well, that turned out to be sort of a dead end," said Simon as they drove away.

Marcie glanced over at him. His lips were pressed tightly together as though he was carefully rationing his words.

"Not completely. We've learned that a man did get a black dog under unusual circumstances."

"You didn't believe his story about the sister-in-law?"

"No. Did you?"

"I guess not. It did seem far-fetched, and five hundred dollars is a lot of money to spend to get a stray dog out of the kennel for your niece. Too bad she couldn't give us a better description of the guy."

"I wonder if the local police have a sketch artist who could draw a picture based on her description."

"Why don't you get Sheila to give the Chief a call? She'll get through to him a lot faster than you will."

Marcie agreed. She took out her cell phone and called Sheila. She gave her a summary of what they'd discovered and asked about the police sketch artist. Sheila quickly agreed to make the call to the Chief.

"Do we have anything scheduled for this afternoon?" asked Simon, staring straight ahead.

"No. I was planning on getting caught up on some of my editing."

"Good. Because Sheila asked me at lunch, while you were out of the room, if I'd like to play nine holes of golf with her at the country club this afternoon. I'm inclined to take her up on it if it doesn't interfere with work."

"Have fun. Are you going right back to Sheila's from the golf course for supper, or are you coming back here?"

"I don't know. How about you call my room around six? If I'm not there, assume that I'm at Sheila's," he said rather curtly.

"Are you okay? Is something bothering you?" Marcie asked.

He twisted around to stare directly at her.

"What bothers me is that none of this is bothering you. We trespassed, found a body, then we lied about why we were looking for that dog. I don't think of that as a particularly uplifting morning."

"We did what we had to do to follow up on the story."

"Well it's more than I signed on for."

"Then don't come along next time."

He continued staring at her, but said nothing.

Marcie left Simon standing by the front desk calling Sheila. As she walked through the lobby headed for the elevator, she heard someone call her name from the direction of the bar.

She turned and saw Steven Pawling loping across the lobby towards her. Still upset from her encounter with Simon, she was in no mood to deal with him.

"I saw you come in and wanted to offer you an apology for my conduct last night," he said.

"You didn't behave badly."

"To be honest, I don't recall how I behaved, but I've learned from the past that usually when I have too much to drink I embarrass myself."

Marcie laughed. "It wasn't that awful."

"Well, then, maybe you'd join me at the bar and I can buy you a drink to make it up to you."

Marcia eyed him warily.

"Don't worry, I'm only drinking club soda. I have a luncheon meeting with Charles today, and after last night, I don't dare show up the least bit impaired."

Smiling, Marcie went with him to the bar where she ordered club soda as well. She studied Steven from the corner of her eye, trying to figure out if Barbara Lieber might have judged him to be in his thirties or forties. She could imagine him being in his early thirties but no older than that. Too bad she couldn't think of a good excuse for taking his picture.

"So you're here to investigate the Jerry Kronberg business?" asked Steven

"Sort of. I'm planning on doing a story on the legend of the black dog and seeing if I can link it to his death."

"Woo! That's spooky."

"It's supposed to be."

"Must be fun writing stories that scare people."

"Yeah, but it's hard to keep finding stuff that's new and scary."

"I've heard about the story of the black dog. That should fill the bill."

Marcie nodded. "I've heard that you own a black dog."

Steven gave her a sidelong glance. "I do, but don't get to thinking that my dog was the one that scared Kronberg. You'll never find me or my dog, Diablo, taking the two mile hike up to

West Peak. A quick walk around the neighborhood is all we can manage."

"How long have you had Diablo?"

"Three years. I got him as a puppy."

"Did you ever have him trained?"

"We tried obedience classes, but it didn't work out. I was more interested in talking to the women than in giving commands, and Diablo spent his time getting friendly with the other dogs. Finally the instructor suggested that neither one of us was ready to be obedient."

Marcie smiled. "Do you know anyone else around here who has a black dog?"

"I don't know anyone else with a black dog, but then nobody other than me brings his dog to the club."

"Another way in which you're disobedient."

"Absolutely. Rules and I just don't get along."

"Is your history of disobedience the reason why your siblings are suing you?"

His face tightened and Marcie thought for a moment that he wouldn't answer, then he seemed to make a conscious effort to relax.

"Actually, investing with Kronberg was one of the few times I played by the rules. I talked to people at the club who know a lot more about investing than I do, and they all advised me that Three Star would be an excellent place to put the family money. So, like a dutiful little boy, I talked my siblings into investing in it.

My brother even came to the club to talk to a couple of the investors, so the idea wasn't just my own. Although you'd think it was by the way my family is distancing themselves from the decision. It's always been easier to blame little Stevie."

"At least you've got yourself a good lawyer."

"Yeah. Charles is a rock. Plus he knows how I feel, because Jerry got his claws into him as well. Misery loves company, as they say."

"Do you think Jerry committed suicide?"

Steve shook his head. "You're asking the wrong guy. I can't imagine taking my own life. When I get down, I just have a couple of drinks and the world seems brighter. But I didn't know Kronberg all that well. Losing all his friends might have hit him pretty hard."

"Are you sure you don't know of anyone else at the country club who owns a black dog?"

The man smiled. "Do you really think Jerry died because of that curse?"

"Maybe not, but I do think he saw a black dog twice on West Peak."

"Well, I don't know of anyone else with a black dog." Steve stopped and gave Marcie a big grin. "Maybe the black dog never comes down from the mountain. Wouldn't that be spooky?"

*****

Amanda entered the restaurant at the inn Richard managed. The young hostess nodded to her and motioned down the hall to the small banquet room. Richard was already there working on his laptop.

"Hi, hon," he said standing up and giving her a gentle kiss on the lips. "I'm sorry we couldn't have lunch together today, but there's a lot going on."

"No problem. I'll only need a few minutes." She sat across the table from him and looked at his smiling face, knowing that she had the power to ruin his spirits. And knowing that was exactly what she was going to do.

"What's wrong? You look nervous."

"I'm calling it off, Richard."

A half smile crossed his face as if he didn't understand what she was saying or thought it was a bad joke.

"Calling what off?"

"Our engagement."

He appeared puzzled, as if something that was usually reliable had suddenly failed to work. This was quickly replaced by the determination to fix the problem.

"I know you were concerned about the date being too soon, but I meant it last time when I said that we could keep it open-ended for a while."

Amanda shook her head. "That wouldn't be fair to you. You'd expect us to get married some day, and I'm not certain that's what I want."

"But why did you agree to marry me, if you didn't want to?"

"There was a whole roomful of people listening; I didn't want to embarrass you."

"You didn't want to embarrass me," he repeated. "How embarrassed do you think I'm going to feel telling my friends and family that our engagement is off before it really got started?"

"I'm sorry. But you shouldn't have asked me in such a public place."

"Do you think I did that on purpose in order to manipulate you into saying 'yes'?"

"Not on purpose. No, I don't think you did it on purpose, but that's the way it turned out."

"So if I asked you right now—in private—to marry me, you would say 'no'?"

Amanda nodded. "I'm not ready to marry you or anyone else."

His face stiffened with disappointment.

Amanda took the ring off her finger and pushed it across the table.

"Maybe you can get your money back on this or sometime in the future you can give it to a woman who truly deserves you."

Richard refused to meet her eyes.

"I hope we can still be friends. Maybe not right now, but in the future."

He didn't say anything, so after waiting a couple of seconds, she turned and walked away.

Chapter 18

When six o'clock came around, Marcie called Simon's room and got no answer. Figuring he was at Sheila's, she drove over there. Sheila answered the door, looking rather somber. She led Marcie down the hall to the living room. Simon was sitting there reading the newspaper. He gave Marcie a curt hello, then resumed reading. Sheila waved Marcie into a chair and then sat down herself.

"Okay," she said in a no-nonsense tone. "I take my food very seriously, and that means I never carry disagreements to the table. I expect my guests to observe the same rules. Simon has told me what happened and why he's upset." She turned to Marcie. "Why don't you tell me your side?"

"It's simple. We found the door unlocked at Wilkie's. I suppose we could have called the police to report an unlocked door and no one responding, but we'd probably still be there now waiting for the police to take it seriously. Lots of people go out and leave their doors unlocked. So technically we trespassed, but we also found a body."

"*I* found a body," Simon added.

"Yes. And I'm sure that was upsetting. We also could have told the truth at the pound, but frankly I'm not sure Tammy would have helped us if we came in with some crazy story about the black dog. I think she might have just sent us on our way. The same goes for visiting the dog owners. The truth might have just gotten us shown the door."

"We should have taken our chances," Simon said. "You've got to have principles or else you're no better than the killers and thieves."

"I do have principles," Marcie said hotly. "None of our lies or other infractions hurt anyone. Everything we did was with the intention of finding out what happened to Kronberg, maybe even to solve a murder."

"That little boy was pretty upset."

"Only for a minute. It's not like we tried to take his dog."

A long moment of silence followed.

"All right. Does anyone feel a strong need to say any more?" Sheila asked and was greeted with silence. "Then we shall put this topic behind us for the rest of the evening? I'm going to heat up what Susan has left for our dinner. Marcie, why don't you give me a hand in the kitchen? Simon, let me tell you where the plates are, and you can set the table."

Twenty minutes later they were sitting at the table with salmon in a light dill sauce in front of them. The aroma of the food reminded Marcie of how hungry she was. The others must have felt the same because everyone ate silently for the first fifteen minutes.

Finally Sheila looked up from her plate and focused on Marcie. "Since Susan isn't here, we can discuss what was discovered today without fear of it spreading around the town. Simon has already filled me in on what you did this morning, so I'll start by telling you what I learned from the Chief this afternoon. He found, after calling everyone on the list of those conned by Three Star, that twelve people had dogs, but that, aside from Pawling's dog, none of them are black, except for one Labrador who is too large and twelve years old, so it's probably not frisky enough to make it up to West Peak."

"Somebody could have an unregistered animal," said Marcie.

"Just what I said to the Chief, but he said that he couldn't spare anyone to visit all forty-three of the people conned to find out if someone might be harboring an unlicensed dog."

"It probably doesn't matter. I think the dog that Barbara Lieber got from the pound for the mystery man is the one," said Marcie. "But how are we going to find out who he is?"

"I talked to the Chief and told him your suggestion about having a sketch artist talk to Lieber. He said that they have an artist who works as a consultant for them, and he'd send him out to see her."

"But even if the sketch does look like someone we know, I'll bet the guy doesn't have the dog anymore. After all, it served its purpose when Kronberg went over the cliff. Keeping it around any longer would be foolish," said Simon

"You might be right," said Marcie. "But if the sketch does fit anyone we know, maybe the Chief could have a lineup or something and see if Lieber can identify the man. It would at least give the police something substantial to go on."

"The only person who is definitely off the hook is Steve Pawling," said Sheila. "He's had that dog for several years."

"Unless he got a second dog from the kennel," said Simon.

"I suppose that's possible, although this whole scheme seems too vicious for Steven," Sheila said. "I don't think he'd kill Jerry. He blames himself for losing the family money more than he blames Jerry."

"What bothers me is that we don't know whether the person behind all of this is one of the people defrauded or a silent partner in the whole scheme," said Simon.

"Or maybe both," Marcie said excitedly, as a couple of pieces of the puzzle slid into place together for her.

"What do you mean?" Sheila asked.

"Well, just think about it. If you were a silent partner in Three Star, wouldn't the best way of diverting attention from yourself be to invest some money with them? That way if the fraud were brought to light, no one would suspect you were a partner if you're among the victims."

"What a clever idea," said Sheila. "It seems almost obvious now that you say it."

"So Ralph Berenson would be the best choice because he was the most aggressive in attacking Kronberg," Simon suggested.

"Maybe too aggressive," Marcie said, waving her fork. "Berenson had been under suspicion from the start because of his harassment of Kronberg. I think it has to be someone else. Someone who's kept a lower profile."

"So what's the killer's motive?" asked Simon.

"What do you mean?" Sheila said.

"Well, what if we say that Kronberg wasn't the only one murdered, but Hunter and Wilkie were also murder victims rather than suicides. Then we have to decide why he did it."

"We'd have to decide whether the killer was someone seeking revenge for having been defrauded or a fourth partner who was afraid that one of the other partners would break down and give his name to the police," said Marcie.

"Exactly," Simon said.

Sheila put down her fork and looked at them incredulously.

"You really think we're talking about a triple murder here?"

"The two suicides took place under suspicious circumstances, and Kronberg's death is an unlikely suicide. So I think we are looking at three murders," said Marcie.

The three people stopped eating and just looked at each other, as if amazed by where their thinking had got them.

On the ride back to the inn that evening, neither Marcie nor Simon said anything. Marcie knew that if she said something apologetic that Simon would probably let bygones be bygones, but Marcie didn't feel it was her place to apologize. She'd just been doing her job. She also was afraid of losing her authority if she said anything that suggested that Simon had been right. Anyway, she thought that Simon should apologize, because it had been her actions that brought them closer to finding the killer. If she'd listened to Simon, they wouldn't have any clue as to who had gotten the black dog. Sometimes you had to stretch the truth a little to get information.

They walked into the inn side by side, saying nothing. They rode up to their floor in the elevator, still silent. They opened the doors to their adjoining rooms without speaking until at the last minute Marcie turned to Simon.

"Tomorrow morning for breakfast?"

He nodded.

Marcie spent the next two hours editing several stories that she'd brought with her on her laptop. Afterwards she called Amanda and updated her on the investigation. Amanda told her about breaking the engagement, and Marcie tried to comfort her by saying that it was for the best. By then it was almost ten o'clock, but she still felt wired from the events of the day. Deciding that she needed some exercise, she got into her bathing suit and headed down to the pool. Aside from a woman at the reception desk, she didn't see anyone on the way. The pool area had a wall of large windows looking out on the parking lot. The darkness outside made it seem warm and cozy inside.

Marcie got in the water and began to swim laps. In a few minutes she could feel the tensions of the day disappearing and her mind drifted off into a meditative state as her body mechanically cut through the water. When she glanced at her waterproof watch, Marcie was surprised to see that a half-hour had elapsed. She took a towel from the cart next to the pool and dried herself off. Then she sat in one of the white plastic chairs and stared out across the pool.

She knew that they'd achieved a lot today. They were well on their way to discovering who'd purchased the black dog, and that meant they were closing in on their killer. Something that Marcie had heard in the last two days was scratching at the back of her mind, but she couldn't bring it fully into her consciousness. She thought it was two pieces of evidence that didn't quite fit together. The more Marcie tried to work it through, the more it danced away, remaining just out of reach. Finally giving up, and hoping that a good night's sleep would help her remember, Marcie pulled on her shorts and T-shirt over her suit and headed back to her room.

There was a stairwell right outside the pool area, so rather than walking all the way back to the lobby to catch the elevator, Marcie decided to take the stairs. She had just reached the landing for the second floor, when the door to the hallway burst open and a figure wearing a ski mask shoved her hard in the chest. Losing her balance, she stumbled backwards down the stairs. Her right hand reached out blindly for the railing, caught it and held on. She felt her wrist twist as she struggled to keep from falling. The figure moved towards her, apparently intent on giving her another push, but just as he got close enough for a shove, Marcie reached forward with her left hand and grabbed her attacker's belt and pulled him towards her. He went flying past her, and bounced awkwardly off the opposite wall. He turned and looked over his shoulder at her for a moment as if undecided whether to resume the attack, then darted off down the stairs.

Marcie didn't move for several seconds, then she sat on the stairs waiting for her heart to stop pounding. She felt her wrist tighten and begin to throb. Finally she went up the stairs and forced herself to open the door to the second floor, still anxious that someone would come bursting through to attack her again. She walked down the hall and went past her room to Simon's where she knocked on his door. She waited, figuring that he most likely was in there. Finally the door opened and Simon stood there in a robe and slippers wiping sleep from his eyes.

"What is it?" he asked.

Marcie opened her mouth but suddenly found herself too choked up to speak. Her eyes filled with tears, and she just stood there for a moment. Startled and not speaking, Simon enveloped her in his arms.

Chapter 19

Marcie thought that Chief Broder looked tired as he sat across the table from her in the inn's empty restaurant, but she wasn't sure whether he was tired because it was midnight or because he was seeing her twice in the same day.

"Could you repeat your description of the man who attacked you?" he asked.

Since she'd already told her story to the two uniformed officers who'd been the first to arrive at the scene after Simon called in the attack, she figured the Chief wanted to make sure she was being consistent in her description of the perpetrator.

"He was tall, over six feet, and on the thin side. He was wearing a ski mask, blue, I think, and a gray sweatshirt, and jeans."

"Did you notice his shoes?"

Marcie shook her head. "I think they were athletic shoes, but I'm not sure."

"He didn't remind you of anyone you've met here in town?"

"No. But I was too busy not getting pushed down the stairs to pay much attention."

"Did he say anything?"

"No. He saved all his energy for pushing me."

The Chief looked down at her right wrist, which was resting in her lap encased in an elastic bandage. "Are you in much pain?"

"I'm fine as long as I don't wave my hand around."

"I heard that the EMTs think it's a mild sprain, but they wanted you to go to the emergency room for an x-ray. However, you refused."

"Maybe I'll go tomorrow. I just couldn't see myself spending half the night waiting to be treated."

The Chief nodded.

"It looks like you're making someone pretty uncomfortable. Maybe there's something in your idea that Kronberg was murdered. Sheila called me yesterday afternoon and told me about this Lieber woman and her dog purchase. I'll have our sketch artist out there this morning to see what we can come up with on this mystery man. You think that he's the one who killed Kronberg?"

"That's right."

"But why the elaborate hoax with the black dog?"

"I think he wanted it to look like Kronberg was becoming unbalanced. Plus it may have helped him to catch Jerry off guard and push him over the cliff."

The Chief looked at her noncommittally, but Marcie decided that she might as well forge ahead with her theory.

"I think this same mystery man is also responsible for the deaths of Jeffrey Hunter and Stanley Wilkie."

The Chief sat back and stared at her for a long moment. "That would tie it all up neatly. But why would this mystery man want to kill the partners in Three Star? Is he an angry investor?"

Marcie shook her head. "I don't think so, although I might be wrong. I think the killer is a fourth partner. Someone who didn't want his name disclosed to the authorities."

"And he was afraid that one or more of the partners might snap during the trial and reveal his identity in order to get a lighter sentence?"

"Exactly."

The Chief took a deep breath. "Even if you're right, we'll probably never be able to prove that the deaths were murders."

"But if we find out who the fourth partner is, you'd be able to check the crime scenes for his fingerprints."

"He probably wore gloves."

"But we'll be able to trace the black dog to him."

"*A black dog*, not necessarily the one Kronberg saw. He and the killer were the only ones present at the time."

"So the killer will never be brought to justice?"

"Hard to say. There are no perfect crimes. So maybe he made some kind of mistake at one of the crime scenes and we'll get him. At least he'll be brought to justice as one of the partners in the Three Star scam."

"Somehow that doesn't seem to be enough punishment for three murders."

"He'll do prison time and his reputation will be shot. It might not be enough, but it won't be just a slap on the wrist either. He might even find out that his plan has backfired because he might get a harsher sentence as the only partner who can be brought to justice."

Marcie was about to say more, but she suddenly felt so tired that all she wanted to do was lie down between clean sheets and sleep.

The Chief must have noticed, because he said, "Why don't you get some rest? I'll call you tomorrow after we've gotten a sketch of our man. Let's hope it looks like someone who's been involved in the case."

Marcie nodded. Saying good night to the Chief, she made her way out into the lobby and pushed the button for the elevator. As she rode up to her room, Marcie began to get the feeling again that something she'd already heard would give her the identity of the mystery man. But delve as she might, she couldn't pull out the piece of evidence she was seeking. This was still on her mind fifteen minutes later when she got into bed and almost immediately fell into a dreamless sleep.

*****

Florence Lee sat at the breakfast nook in her bright, sunny kitchen and listened to the sounds of the house. She couldn't hear her housekeeper and confidant, Mrs. Eldridge, who was clearing the bedrooms upstairs. She must not be using the vacuum yet, she thought to herself. I think we should get a new vacuum. Mrs. Eldridge isn't getting any younger and the old vacuum is heavy to push around this large house. She got up to pour herself a second cup of coffee, when the phone on the kitchen wall began to ring. She answered and suddenly her attention was fully focused on what she was hearing. After listening for several moments, she agreed to what was being asked.

Immediately after hanging up the phone, she went in search of Mrs. Eldridge, finally finding her cleaning the master bathroom.

"Mrs. Eldridge," she said.

She would have happily called her by her first name, Sarah, but she knew Mrs. Eldridge would continue to address her formally. So to keep things on a footing of equality, she was equally formal.

Mrs. Eldridge looked up from the inside of the bathtub that she was scouring.

"I've just received a call from a man who refused to identify himself. He says that he has information about a fourth partner in Three Star."

A raised eyebrow indicated Mrs. Eldridge's surprise.

"He says he'll give me the information proving this person's involvement if I meet him alone at West Peak."

"Surely you don't plan to do that," Mrs. Eldridge said.

"I do plan to meet with him, but not alone. I think I'll call Ralph Berenson and ask him to accompany me."

Mrs. Eldridge looked doubtful. "Perhaps it would be better to call the police."

Florence paused, pretending that she was taking the advice into consideration.

"I can't see the police sending a couple of officers scrambling up to West Peak, and even if they did, my informant would probably just disappear and never contact me again. I should be quite safe with Berenson along."

"He doesn't seem to me to be the most physically prepossessing of men."

"True, he's small but he's very wiry, and I know he's climbed to the top of West Peak before."

"But wouldn't the two of you appearing on the Peak still scare off your informant?"

"I'll have him hike up a few minutes behind me. He can observe our meeting from a place of concealment, but be ready to help me if I require assistance."

Mrs. Eldridge's expression remained doubtful, but she knew that there was no point in disagreeing with her employer once she had determined on a course of action. So she simply nodded and went back to her cleaning.

*****

Marcie was waiting in the lobby for Simon, so they could go in to breakfast. She'd wisely set her alarm, certain that otherwise she'd still be asleep. As it was, Marcie felt pretty rested considering that she'd only gotten four hours of sleep. The elevator doors opened and Simon came out. He saw her and smiled.

"How are you feeling this morning?"

"Pretty good, considering."

"I would have waited for you to be done last night, but the police just about ordered me to return to my room. When did you get to bed?"

"A little after two."

"And you're down here at seven-thirty looking pretty chipper. That's quite an accomplishment."

Marcie nodded. She knew that she had to say something to Simon about their disagreement. Last night he'd been so supportive when she came to his door, that she wanted things to be right between them.

He started to head toward the dining room, but she touched his arm to stop him.

"I just wanted to apologize for the way I acted yesterday. I shouldn't have insisted you come along on anything that made you feel uncomfortable."

Simon smiled. "Well, I owe you an apology, too. After all, you've got a lot more experience in things like this. If I didn't want to do something, I should have just said so instead of calling your ethics into question and then pouting like a little girl. And you were right, if you hadn't acted as you did, we wouldn't be nearly as far along on the investigation as we are."

"And although I may not admit it to Amanda, it was really nice having someone along to share my opinions with and to turn to for support," Marcie said.

"I couldn't imagine doing this on my own," Simon agreed.

When they were seated at their table and the waitress had brought them coffee, Marcie told Simon what she'd told the Chief last night.

"Did he agree with you?"

"He didn't disagree. I think he likes it as a hypothesis, but isn't sure how much of it he'll ever be able to prove."

"It would be a shame if a triple murderer got off scot free," Simon said, taking a sip of his coffee. "I feel particularly bad about Kronberg because he does seem to have had some sense of decency."

"What are you thinking about?"

"The fact that he refused to sell shares in Three Star to his friend Lloyd Schmidt."

Marcie sat for a moment staring across the room, then her eyes opened wide.

"That's it," she almost shouted.

"What's it?" Simon looked quickly around the room.

"The inconsistency I've been trying to remember. I find it hard to believe that Kronberg wouldn't cheat his best friend, Lloyd Schmidt, but that he'd con his brother-in-law."

"You don't think Charles Foster was actually a victim?"

"Oh, I'm sure his name is on the list of investors and that he put some money into the company. But I think he did it intentionally, so if anything went wrong, no one would ever think of him as a silent partner."

"As a supposedly reputable lawyer, he certainly wouldn't want to be exposed as part of the scam."

"Oh, I think he was part of it all right. In fact, I think he was probably the brains of the operation. Remember Getz saying that he couldn't believe those three guys could come up with a plan like that. They probably didn't, but Charles Foster did."

"So does that mean Charles Foster is the one who attacked you last night?" asked Simon.

"Yes. We know he was here earlier in the day when he was with Steve Pawling. Maybe he even took a room in the inn near ours to keep an eye on us. And I think he was also the driver of the car that tried to run me down. I'll bet he's been following us around ever since we came to town, looking for an opportunity to frighten us into leaving."

"But how are we going to prove all of this?"

Marcie sipped her coffee then shook her head.

"I think we should get in touch with Florence Lee. She's been searching for the fourth partner all along. Maybe she can think of some way to build a case against Foster."

Marcie pulled her notebook out of her pocket and leafed through it. When she found Lee's number, she punched it into her cell phone. After a few rings, the phone was answered by a Mrs. Eldridge, who identified herself as the housekeeper, and said that Mrs. Lee wasn't home.

"Can I reach her on her cell phone?" Marcie asked.

"Her phone was dead, so she left it here," Mrs. Eldridge replied.

"We really need to reach her. It's about the Kronberg case."

The woman paused as if uncertain what to say. "The two of you were here the other day, right? You're that writer for a magazine."

"Yes."

"Normally I wouldn't tell you this, but I'm concerned that Mrs. Lee may be doing something that's dangerous." She then went on to tell Marcie about the phone call and the meeting planned at West Peak.

"How long ago did Mrs. Lee leave?"

"About fifteen minutes. The meeting is scheduled for eleven o'clock, and it takes about two hours to hike up to the Peak."

After thanking the woman, Marcie turned to Simon.

"Did you bring any hiking gear?"

He gave her a puzzled look. "I do have a pretty sturdy pair of walking shoes."

"They'll have to do. I'll wear my running shoes. Let's go."

"But we haven't eaten our breakfast yet."

"No time. Get ready and I'll meet you in the lobby in ten minutes. I'll fill you in on the drive."

Half an hour later they were standing at the foot of a trail that the ranger at the front gate of Hubbard Park had told them was the fastest route to West Peak.

"Looks kind of rugged," said Simon, staring up at the rocky ascent. "I'm not sure I'm up to a two hour hike uphill. Shouldn't we just call the police?"

"No crime has been committed yet. And anyway, by the time the Comford police work things out with the Meriden police and the park authorities, it will be too late. We'll just have to do our best," said Marcie, beginning to climb.

After a half-hour they stopped for a rest. Although it was a cool April morning, Marcie took off her sweatshirt and tied it around her waist. The T-shirt underneath was already damp from exertion. They both took a drink from the bottle of water each was carrying. Simon had taken off one shoe and was looking inside it.

"Something in there is rubbing," he said, dumping out a couple of pebbles. "You said this is a two hour climb?"

"At least. About four miles. We've probably come a mile and a half already."

He took out a handkerchief and rubbed it over his bald head.

"Too bad I don't have a hat. At this rate I'll get a sunburn."

Marcie checked her watch. "We'd better get going. It's ten and the meeting is scheduled for eleven. We're going to be late as it is."

"She'll have Berenson with her, that should keep her safe."

"Foster has already killed three men. We shouldn't underestimate him."

They resumed climbing. Marcie found herself getting into a rhythm as she followed the trail upward. At some points it was steep enough that she felt the muscles burn in her legs, but she pushed on and the trail eventually evened out. She slowed down several times to let Simon catch up. He was getting very red in the face and his breath was ragged. Marcie knew that they couldn't go on like this much longer, and she had, if anything, to pick up the pace if she was going to reach West Peak anywhere close to the meeting time.

"Did you hear something?" Simon called out ten minutes later.

Marcie paused. There was a loud thrashing coming from behind a large bush just off the side of the trail. At first she thought it was a big animal, and they should get out of the area quickly. But before she could say anything, a human form staggered out of the woods and onto the trail right in front of them. It was Ralph Berenson. The collar of his shirt was bright red with blood, and he stood there looking about himself with a dazed expression. Simon grabbed him by both shoulders and stared into his eyes.

"Are you all right?"

"I know you," Berenson said in a fuzzy voice.

"What happened?" Simon asked.

The man lost his balance and almost slipped from Simon's grasp.

"Who did this to you?" Simon shouted.

"Don't know. Hit me from behind."

"Where's Florence Lee?" asked Marcie.

"Yes, Florence," he said and drifted off.

Simon gave Berenson a drink of water, and he slowly seemed to revive.

"Florence wanted me to follow behind, so the man she was going to meet wouldn't know she hadn't come alone. She was about ten minutes ahead of me."

"But the guy was watching you both from the time you arrived, so he trailed behind you and took you out when he had the chance," said Marcie.

Berenson stared at her intently, but didn't respond.

Marcie turned to Simon, "You stay with him. Make your way up to the Peak, but go as slowly as you have to. Call the police and tell them someone has been assaulted on the trail, that should get some action."

"What are you going to do?" Simon asked.

"Move as fast as I can to catch up with Florence," Marcie said, turning and heading up the trail.

She picked up speed. Soon her breath was getting rapid, and she could feel her heartbeat in her ears. Her injured wrist began to hurt as she pulled on branches to hurry herself along. Marcie was working so hard that it came as a surprise when she climbed up a small hill and suddenly found herself at the top of the mountain. Off to her left, the city of Meriden was spread out before her. In front of her was an open area surrounded by trees. About fifty yards away two people were talking: Charles Foster and Florence Lee. As they talked, Marcie could see that Foster was leading Florence in a seemingly meandering stroll, but one which brought them ever closer to the edge of the cliff.

Marcie began to walk quickly, gradually diminishing the distance between the couple and herself.

Their backs were to her, so when she called out 'Hello there,' they both spun around in surprise.

"Oh, hello, Ms. Ducasse, I'm glad that you're here," Florence Lee said. "Mr. Foster was about to give me some information about the fourth partner in Three Star."

"I doubt that very much," Marcie said, walking up to them.

Florence looked puzzled. "Why would you say that?"

Charles Foster looked at her, a small smile on his face. "Yes, why would you say that?"

"Because you are the fourth partner in Three Star. And you are also responsible for the deaths of your three partners."

"You have no evidence of that," Foster said.

"I'll bet I have enough to get federal prosecutors to go through your e-mails. I bet they'll find something linking you to Three Star now that they know where to look."

Foster reached behind his back and a gun appeared in his hand. He waved it, indicating that Marcie should stand next to Florence.

I'm going to give the two of you a choice; you can take your chances and jump off the cliff or you can stay where you are and get shot."

"You wouldn't shoot us," Marcie said hoarsely, her mouth suddenly dry. "You've tried all along to make the deaths look like suicides. No one is going to think we committed suicide."

Foster smiled. "Maybe not, but no one would associate your deaths with me. Berenson never saw me when I hit him, so no one knows I'm here."

Marcie considered telling him that Simon knew, but she was afraid that Foster would just wait on the Peak and kill Simon and Berenson when they appeared.

"Why did you do it?" Marcie asked, trying to win more time. "You were a successful lawyer.

Why would you get mixed up in a Ponzi scheme?"

"Yes, I was a successful lawyer. A lawyer to the really rich, something I would never be. And every day I became more and more convinced that I was smarter and more capable then any of them. So I worked out an investment con and got my gullible brother-in-law to be the front man, and, sure enough, these smart, rich people lined up to get fleeced. But when it all came tumbling down, the three guys that I had made rich wanted to turn me in so they could get lighter sentences. That was something I just couldn't allow to happen."

"And what about the black dog? I know you got one from the pound. Lieber will identify you to the police."

Foster shrugged. "All she can prove is that I had a black dog. She didn't see me spend hours training it to obey my commands or see me hide up here in the woods teaching the dog to run toward the cliffs and then return to me. She wasn't here to see the expression on Jerry's face when he saw the dog running towards him for the third time. He was so scared that it was easy for me to push him off the cliff."

"Do you still have the dog?" I asked.

Foster shook his head. "He's buried where no one will ever find him."

"You're a terrible man, to kill a dog," Florence said.

Foster smiled at her coldly, then Marcie saw his gaze drift off to some point behind her. His expression became very intense, then even fearful. He stepped around Marcie and raised his gun. Marcie turned and from out of the woods she saw a black dog coming. Running without making a sound and almost seeming to float above the ground. Foster raised his gun and began to fire. He kept firing until he ran out of ammunition, but the dog kept coming. He turned as if to run, then he clutched his chest and fell to the ground. As quickly as it had appeared, the dog disappeared back into the woods.

Florence Lee rolled Foster onto his back and began doing chest compressions. When she got tired Marcie took over until Florence tapped her on the shoulder and shook her head.

Chapter 20

That night Marcie lay on her bed at the inn with the phone to her ear for over twenty minutes filling Amanda in on what had happened. That included the final chapter when a park ranger led two fit police officers to West Peak, where they found the two women and Simon and Berenson. They improvised a litter to carry Foster's body down from the mountain.

"So was it a stray dog that just happened along or *the* black dog?" Amanda asked.

"I don't know, but it certainly disappeared right after Foster fell to the ground."

"One thing I don't understand," Amanda said, "is why Foster died. He'd only seen the real black dog for the first time. According to the legend, that shouldn't have been enough to kill him."

"Maybe it was the ghost of the dog he'd killed, seeking vengeance. Or you could say that he saw the black dog four times. Three times when he frightened Kronberg, and then the last time when he died. I don't know. Either way it makes for a great story. But I do know that having seen the black dog once, I'm never going to hike there again and risk seeing it for a second time."

"Talking about second times," Amanda said, "Richard and I are back together again."

"Not engaged?"

"No. But Richard came over last night and convinced me that we should start going out together again. I think he feels that if he works at it long enough eventually I'll marry him."

"Do you think he's right?"

"Well, I have to say, I'm impressed by the fact that he's sticking with me. And I do love the guy."

"But you're just not ready to get married?"

"The question is whether I'll ever be. How did things go with Simon?"

"Up and down, like any couple," Marcie said with a laugh. "Actually he's not coming back with me, he's staying down here at Sheila Little's house for a few days."

"Wow, he works fast."

"Somebody does, but I think it may be Sheila."

"How's he going to get back up here? His car is in our parking lot."

"I'm sure Sheila will find a way."

"Well, drive safely, and I'll see you bright and early the day after tomorrow."

After she hung up, Marcie looked across the room and smiled contentedly. She was already composing the story in her head.

ABOUT THE AUTHOR

 Glen Ebisch is the author of *The Black Dog*, the latest in the Marcie and Amanda Mystery series. A recently retired professor of philosophy, he has had a number of mysteries for young adults and adults published over the past twenty-five years. He currently resides with his wife in western Massachusetts where he practices yoga and writes mysteries.